I0453740

THE ONLINE DATER

Jeffrey Ellinger

Copyright © 2015 Jeffrey Ellinger
All rights reserved.
ISBN-13: 9780692481226
ISBN: 0692481222

TO ROBIN

CHAPTER ONE

I am being driven by an unknown power. I am being forced to purge my mind. So when it's out, all bare and gross, I will have told the story of everything that happened, and that will protect me from future mistakes. It's crazy, I know, but I'm to the point where it's crazier to not do this, which I know also sounds crazy.

This sort of diseased thinking must be impossible to avoid. If a failure goes on long enough, it has to be. Though even as I recognize my psychosis, it seems unsettling to believe, as I do now, my phone has stopped receiving messages from numbers its robot brain has chosen.

What's worse yet, as I lie here and wonder, is I think she may have lost her phone. That as she was pressing send, she walked over a storm grate and it slipped through her fingers, fell through the rungs. Now she is without my number. I should text her. I should make sure everything is okay. I have to.

A stream of common sense leaks in my brain. Patience runs through my mind. I set down my phone. I wait. The television is on. A Mexican man with white teeth and thick hair is training bad dogs to be good dogs. This man is ten years older than I am, and I want his hair so badly.

Though I would forgo even my deepest fantasy, of having hair like his, if it meant my phone lighting up right now. Again I pick it up. I open and close it, over and over I do this, vacant of any thought beyond willing this device to receive a message. I've done this many times before, enough the hinges have become worn.

But nothing is coming, and my insides grind as I construct the scenario of what she is doing. She is drinking a beer, laughing with her roommates and scrolling through Facebook. She is on a bike ride with another man…and right before I see them in bed, I stop. Please God, please for a second make her appreciate a sliver of this. Help her find a way outside of the artificial world we entered. Help us show mercy to one another.

Days have passed since I last heard from her. Husbands and wives have kissed each other hundreds of times in that span. Babies have been born. I know I should give up on an excuse, something like, "Robert, things are just really busy right now." I should get up and dust myself off. Go online and update my profile. Get to the gym. Find a better job. Take pictures of myself highlighting my eyes, which I have been told can be attractive, and my skin, which is clear for now, but not my hair, which I am sure I must have been misleading women into believing I have more of… but now, a message.

No, right away, no. This will not be her. This is a picture message, and she would never send a picture message. This will be from my mom. Maybe an eagle she spotted in the country, or one of my dad's cows. Picture messages from those who are not in my family—the ones like unopened presents in my inbox—have dwindled. All those fit backsides inside fashionably-cut underwear, hands cupping breasts, red mouths slightly open, were never saved, and now fade from memory. Even if I had not deleted them, if I could open my phone and look at those forms now, they would not make me glad. They would only act as a reminder of what I once had but can never have again.

The message, opening finally, is from my brother-in-law. This is his daughter. Her blonde hair all wet, curls dangling down her precious head. She is in her pajamas, smiling, showing off the gap where she lost one of her two front teeth. And that is good, to see my family healthy and happy. Still I am disappointed. I cannot see my niece in her cozy home in the country with her nurse mother and her engineer father without wishing she was a woman I hardly know. I prefer someone who will not call me back over someone who has drawn me beside a unicorn under a rainbow. I prefer someone I have seen twice, and when I asked for a third time she said she needed to "feel out our dynamic," over a person who gives me a sweet kiss whenever I see her.

I should have wowed this stranger more. I should have inspired her to delete her profile. She would've then changed the programmed name in her phone from Robert OkC to Robert. She would've responded to my message sent two days ago, going on three. I should give up on all that. I know this, but I am unable to convince myself of our disproportionate heart-states.

Our first time together, I arrived at a lake in our city of Minneapolis on a warm afternoon in late spring, on vacation from my job producing generic drugs. It is true, I am just a man who works in a factory, though I am doing alright. I recently traveled to Europe, and I have a steady job. I live in a neighborhood with the good bars and restaurants. These things are the important things, they say. Though it is possible no one cares about anything beyond looks and money. I have no idea. Let me stick to what I know, our day at the lake.

Megan arrived by bicycle, which is how she got everywhere. I do not get anywhere by bicycle, nor do I buy my food at co-ops. And I definitely do not have, like she has, a degree in sustainable agriculture and community planning. Differences aside, even before we met, I believed we could be something. I constructed our relationship in my mind. Her name was Megan. My first love was the same, and though I had grown since, beginning to know that name as a name for athletic high schools girls, I still thought we might be something. I could become a man who wore tights in bars without being self-conscious of my testicles.

Megan greeted me with a handshake and a bright hello, then a small awkward chuckle. We were smiling like a great team already as we went on our walk, and soon came the nagging hope. It overtook me as I heard the click-clacking of her biking shoes against the paved walking path. And as I breathed in the freshness of the lake, I thought, though we do not know each other, we could love each other someday.

I wish I could say I thought something mundane like "she seems nice, I wonder if she likes Bergman movies" but I did not. I thought about falling in love. Which made me nervous, and that made me begin to babble. I would have rather been terse, as I imagine my father was when he first dated my mother. But I never am. I babble, explaining how I've become more of this and not more of something else. I do that to show my potential, rather than my reality. The problem—for those my age—is that potential is a fickle, transient thing. We want a yard, soon. Pets, maybe sooner. And while some never say it, we want someone who can support a child, when the time comes. Knowing these things, I feel for those who sign into the dating website and read or send messages. They must wonder why their friends are attached and taking adorable pictures in scenic areas then posting them to social media and not them.

I babble, as I babbled with Megan. I did stop eventually, somewhere after the wood bridge where two boys fished. Megan began to relay a recent bike trip through the mountains of Colorado. I didn't say to her then—maybe she could sense it—but there will never be a point in my life when I bike up mountains. I will never advance the genetic pool with large calves and atrophied arms. I have a capable body, just not a tubular one, hollow as a bird. Megan described the mountain climb anyway: breath leaving her, lungs shrinking, throat tightening. But it was all fake drama, the ending secured. It was when she said something else that I perked up.

"He's my trip buddy," Megan said in a Northern Wisconsin accent. She had on biking shorts and a tank top. Mascara ran in a sharp line away from her eye. "He calls me out of the blue and we just go. North Carolina, Montana, Colorado. He's like a high-up at *Trek* and sets up expos, so he's always taking these kinds of trips."

I smiled, pretending to enjoy Megan's story, but I could have not heard one more thing about the man's trailer or how fast he could go on his customized bike or how many locally grown meals he bought her, I could have not heard any of that and lived well.

"I was just so tired when we were done," Megan finished. "All I could do was lay on the hotel bed and stare at the ceiling."

I believed her when said that, in a general sense. Megan and the man had two beds and that was the bed she chose to lie on at that particular moment. Later, though, when I allowed honesty to enter in my brain, I understood it was her bed. It was his bed. It was their bed.

But I was too blinded by the possibility of us. We had found a spot on the grass close to the beach on the first real day of warmth, and we began to talk about our parents. Mine planned to visit soon. I confided in Megan that I would not know what to talk about for three full days.

"I might have to bare my soul," I said, and that made Megan smile. It seemed to brighten our shade.

"Really?" she asked.

"I mean, who knows," I said, tossing individual blades of grass. "I just don't know what to say most of the time. How much can you really tell your parents? When my dad calls, he gives me this rundown on all the people who've died in my hometown. What do you say to that?"

"My dad tells me about that kind of stuff too." Megan was in agreement. She looked out near the lake where two boys kicked a soccer ball. I took the time to admire her small breasts. On the walk I noticed she had a bottom which should not be joked about. I picked off the heads of three dandelions and arranged them on her bruised legs. She had fallen while in Colorado.

"What's going on there?" she asked, and I almost stopped.

"This is art, Megan. Please, don't disturb the artist." Her smile acted as an appeasement, and I placed the green sticks on her legs, making tiny stacks. The tips of my fingers glanced against her freshly-shaven legs. We talked about her phone next, whether, because it was very new, it should be considered a "science" or "space" phone.

That was the first time, then we had the next time at the same lake. I went early, and as sat on the gravely-brown sand, the sun waning over the sheltering trees, I heard sounds of children playing. I began to read a book. A group of young women arrived before Megan. They found their spot on the beach and took their clothes off to swim. For one of them, along with her shirt came her swimming top, and though I pretended to not look at her breasts, free as Eve's in the Garden, my eyes were well above the pages of my book. There was laughter as the woman—her top expertly slipped back on—and her friends ran out to the water. Kicking up sand and shouting like schoolgirls, they seemed happy. I was too, I think. That afternoon, I was.

Megan came by bicycle again, this time already wearing a bikini bottom with a t-shirt. I try to play it back now, the way her backside peeked out of her suit. It's likely, this very day, a man is near it and can touch it whenever he wants. What an awful thing to know.

After we finished swimming, we lounged on the sand as the shade of the trees crept in on us. Music played from Megan's phone. Towel beneath her, her head down, I worked the muscles along her shoulder blades.

"You're so going to make me fall asleep," she said, and I thought this: there will never be a time when I am anxious with you. I will rub your back when we're old, even when it's not as perfect, age spots and moles and wrinkles, I will rub this back and I will love it, because it will be yours.

Soon enough, our time expired, but before we left I asked Megan if she wanted to come over.

"We could enjoy the day a bit longer," I said. "Maybe grill?"

And she nearly did, I think. She nearly skipped her bike meeting. Megan had a bike ride or a bike cause to support every night, but after I explained to her the grass-fed beef I had, given to me by my father, she nearly did. "We could just sit outside on the porch and drink beers," I added, without longing, I hope. But I have to think now a pathetic streak ran down my face like sweat.

"That sounds nice," she said, "but I should go. I need to sign up for things." So we gathered up our belonging-ness and went to where she parked her bike. We had a kiss. Not a long or a particularly lust-filled one, but it was good. Then she biked away.

Which brings me to now, and even with these days of her silence behind us, I have hope. As if I cannot bring myself to reality, as if every last strand has to be cut and burned and those ashes have to be shot into space, gone in every direction of the galaxy. I know I should not be sitting here staring at a phone and doubting its viability. I should have better things to do. I should not...*a message*. This is it. This is her number. I open my phone slowly. I peel one eye open at a time. Her words are manna.

"Robert, hey, it's been great getting to know you. You're a nice guy. But I don't see anything further between us. Best of luck, Megan."

I know for others this text is nothing, maybe so insignificant they would forget as soon as they closed their phone. They might shrug their shoulders and go eat pizza.

I lie back down on the couch, aware of everything around me. My mind hurtles as I begin to remember these last years. How each new time I believed everything would be different and how it never was. I remember the one who would have steered me away from these memories. More and more, I remember her.

CHAPTER TWO

The snow storm did not make her late. Hannah was already seated by the time I got there. The waitress pointed to our booth and I saw the back of her head. The hair that would become familiar: dark, in heavy bunches. Probably curly as a child, now, as a woman, wavy and dense.

"Hannah?" I said, making her turn toward me, in some way forcing her to smile. Which she did, though it crumbled as soon as it came.

"Sorry I'm late," I said as I sat down.

"That's okay," she said. "Just got here."

I took off my coat, stuffed it between myself and the wall, and looked at her for the first time. What I felt, I can't say for certain, though I know I was overtaken with what I thought. Not with a word like cute, as if Hannah were petite and had pixie bangs. Or with hot—like the wife of a professional baseball player—or even beautiful. She was pretty. She had clear brown eyes and full lips, and an attractive Jewish nose, Hannah was very pretty.

Her coat, hung up on the booth's hanger to our left, was yellow, with rainbow stripes around the shoulders. "That's your coat?" I asked, taking off my stocking hat. Hannah seemed warm in the seat across from me.

"Colorful, isn't it?"

"Definitely colorful," I said. And because I did not know what else to say, I just repeated that. "Definitely colorful."

Hannah gave me another smile, the same as our first one, and I hoped she was not annoyed. She was so pretty. "What are you thinking of getting?" she asked. Coffee steam swirled out of her cup.

"Boy," I said as I opened up a menu, "I don't know. What's good?"

"Everything's good here. I wouldn't have come if it wasn't." And she winked. It seemed to forgive me for being late. But I still had to say something.

"I'm sorry," I said, putting the menu down. "Was it a bad drive? I was surprised at how much it was snowing when I walked out. I wanted to call you, but…."

"Rob, really, don't worry. It wasn't bad."

"Well, that's good to hear. But I am sorry."

"It's not a problem, honestly. So do you go by Rob, or Robert?" Hannah did not want to linger on anything unpleasant.

"Rob's good, but I don't mind Robert. Some of my good friends call me that."

"Robert," she said, as if memorizing it. "I like that. Robert"

"Robert and Hannah," I said and stamped down my menu jauntily, thinking nothing of the future. "We've decided what we should call each other. Now we can eat."

She kind of laughed—but not too much because it wasn't funny—and soon the waitress came. I ordered an omelet and pancakes and Hannah got strawberry crepes, which she let me take a bite of, and they were, like she said they would be, delicious. I became sated with the portions, but more full with possibilities as I learned about Hannah. She was in her final semester at the University of Minnesota, earning her MFA with an emphasis in sculpture. We discussed her art more than anything else, and I liked that. I worked at a factory and enjoyed sports and movies. I was dull in comparison. Nearer the end, we began to flirt, talking about old boy-friends and girlfriends, a topic which always seems to be a road to somewhere else.

"So," she said, her bangs falling over her olive-skinned forehead, paler from the long winter. "What kind of girl is your type?"

I never had a type, I thought. "A type, I guess I just like when I meet a pretty girl…" I looked up. "…who has a good heart." I could tell Hannah did. "Someone who laughs at the things I say."

"But what about blondes or brunettes," she said. "Anything like that?"

"I think the last girl I dated with blonde hair was in high school." I put the napkin over the scraps of my meal. "How about you, what's your type?"

"Actually, my three last boyfriends have been stocky bald guys with beards." And she turned her eyes up toward me for emphasis. I knew what she was saying, by not saying anything more, but I did not like to think of myself as bald, I just shaved my head. And I didn't like to think of myself as stocky, I just needed to go to the gym. And I didn't like to think of myself as bearded, I just happened to not shave.

"Sounds like you've dated some handsome men," I said anyway.

We both blushed, and she changed the subject, "Do you know if there's a Home Depot close?" Neither of us had smartphones.

"Not sure," I said, but I didn't want the morning to end, so I added, "If you want, you could come over and we could look it up? I don't live very far from here."

"That'd be fine," she said. Like that, she followed me to my place.

In just a few minutes her yellow coat was draped over a couch in a living room in the suburbs where I lived instead of a hanger in a restaurant, and the TV had been turned on to a daytime soap opera as she searched for the *Home Depot*. We sat close. A burly mess of chest hair filled the TV, just rising out of a hot tub all steamy, and at that moment we both happened to look up and share a laugh. Then it became quiet. We turned and kissed. Slowly at first, then more and more. Afterward, as she was putting her shirt back on, I could tell I had spoiled my jeans.

"Wow," she said. "You were ready."

"Oh, I. I didn't mean…"

"…No no, Rob, it was good. But I should get going."

"Of course," I said, "right. Right." So I guided Hannah to the side door of the house where I lived in the suburbs with an old friend I called my landlord. A cat lived with us. I worked in the late afternoon into the early evening at a factory that produced generic pharmaceuticals. Nearby, the driveway was white from snow. More came down. I feared I would never see Hannah again.

"So," she said. It was ending. That's how last conversations start, with that word. Then she floored me. "Next time. Thai?"

"Thai," I said like I'd been punched, just cogent enough to give thanks to whoever made miraculous things happen. "Definitely."

We kissed at the doorway, then she walked away down the driveway wearing her yellow coat with the rainbow stripes. And I wish I could say, like some kind of sappy song, that as I watched her go, she moved into my heart. I wish.

CHAPTER THREE

Months before Hannah was Natalie Gardner. My first online date. She is now famous, in a local way. Natalie has a band here in Minneapolis, and they play around town—and the country more and more—and one publication or another has an article on her band every other month, it seems. So in a way, at least when they're looking to sell records, I am forced to remember her name.

When we met, it was different. She was in her early twenties—half-white half-Spanish, with wild curly hair—and showed up to the pizza place twenty minutes late, jerking to a halt in a Buick Regal filled to the brim with "junk," she explained before I had time to say anything else, she was in the process of moving from one loft with her friends to another loft, probably with even more.

It should be said before going further that women judge as men judge in those first moments. If I am older or more bald or overweight in real life, that is taken account of and stored away until whenever we may part, which has been sooner, rather than later, if I am less than my pictures. That is how it is. So as soon as Natalie got out of her car, and though I could tell she was full of good energy, she was not what I thought she would be. I could never see her again for the first time.

We ate. I told her about my job, where I worked in a position less impressive than it is now - and it is not impressive now - though Natalie seemed happy I had something at all. For the most part, I listened to her talk about herself and her family - in Texas and Wisconsin - and her friends starting a band.

"I might do some backup singing," she told me.

That was a Sunday, and I had recently moved to Minneapolis. I did not know the city. Natalie wanted to show it to me. She asked if she could.

"That'd be great," I told her after as we stood by her car. I left a liar. I would not respond to the messages she sent, not that night or the next few days.

Now it is years later and I hardly recognize her in the band photos she's part of, the ones taken for alt-weeklies.

She is much slimmer, with a modern haircut—shaved on one side—and so many tattoos.

Seeing her like that, in one particular picture online where her breasts seemed to pulsate, I got so proud I once went on a date with her, I pathetically dug out her old number and texted her to say, "Congrats on the album. By the way, you look great."

Maybe she changed numbers, I can tell myself now, but that kind of thinking is similar to the kind of thinking which leads one to believe their phone is self-aware and blocking messages from numbers it knows its master wants to see because the phone is interested in schadenfreude. No, this story of Natalie—the first I met while online dating—is another normal online dating story. It just so happened to be my first one.

CHAPTER FOUR

We saw other people then, neither of us yet sold on the idea of spending the rest of our lives with someone we met on the internet. And though she never said, I like to believe Hannah came close to that. I like to think she would have been content to have only me.

I did later learn of a Jewish boy who Hannah told me her mom would've been "really happy about," and another fellow, an Indian man. Hannah saw them after our morning of pancakes, which surprised me at the time, though no longer. It's what everyone does, even if we meet someone attractive and special and tender and all the things we would ever want in another person, we continue on the march, seeing more and more people, as if we are robots trained to do so, and to deviate from the plan, to discontinue from the neverending queue of new flesh in our inbox would be a sin, one that would lead us away from that one real true love and directly into the settling arms of a lesser one.

A weekday night, a short time after pancakes, Hannah said she would come down to seem me in the suburbs, but first I had to get off work from a factory in the northwest suburbs of Minneapolis that produced generic pharmaceuticals. I wore a white lab coat there, even if the job had little to do with science and everything to do with how well one can watch small bottles of medicine go by a conveyor belt as they make sure the small bottles of medicine have a label, then to put those small bottles of medicine into a box, and wrap that box and stack it on a pallet.

This kind of assembly line work is not as whimsical as one might imagine from television, though I don't mind it. It pays well enough I can afford to bring home a decent bottle of wine, a large piece of stilton, or even some dark chocolate, without thinking twice. Those luxuries must be why one will put up with what one puts up with at a job.

That night, years ago, Hannah and I drank the wine and ate the chocolate, the cheese with crackers too, as we watched television on my landlord's couch. When we began to take off our clothes, she offered we go upstairs, and I agreed, though I knew it would not be great. I am never great the first time.

But that night is the night I learned how good Hannah would be. There have been other times by now where the same thing has happened and the person I tried to fulfill has moved on without speaking a word on why. Hannah must have envisioned me as more than a man with a job at a factory and a member not so ready off the bat and a face which must be hard to love, as I have always been in and out of it. I could have married her for those reasons.

"It's okay," she said. I was lying on the mattress, sweating. She wiped my brow, her hair dangling like cords of soft dark ribbon. "But is everything…okay?"

My hands over my chest, I said, "Definitely, I just, you know, have a tougher time the first time. I feel like I should know someone."

Hannah let her body rest on mine. "Oh my gosh, Robert. Are we moving too fast?"

"No-no. This is good. I'll get better. It will." I think Hannah believed what I told her. I thought so by the way she situated herself, curling up, her head resting on me.

"I love this," she said as she swirled it with her fingers. "I never liked chest hair before, but I like yours."

I kissed the top of her head. Her right leg draped over mine, we did not speak. I listened to her drift away.

CHAPTER FIVE

The one after Natalie had a Christian name and also a nickname. My friend in Chicago gave it to her after I told him what she and I had done. He called her Ballsucker. I love my friend. I believe what he made up was his way of describing the proclivities he would want to see in his wife. A name like Ballsucker may seem inflammatory, but it was not an insult. It was a celebration.

Problematically, though, regurgitating it, or the ones other online daters use to sum up the ones they meet—"Big Balls," "Tiny Nipples," "Stinky Pits," and so on—is no way to curb the degradation of humanity plaguing those very same online daters. Today, hundreds more will be given. One must stop and use the name given at birth.

Hers was a good name. Sara, who wore fake pearls and referenced Russian novelists and had a way about her. Sara with the curved mouth and oceanic eyes, you could see her vivacious nature without meeting her. I wanted to meet her. I was on the website for that very reason, so I messaged her. Why she answered is not important, unless one day we would have married. These messages, I like to think mine are more charming than others, though I am positive it would alarm me to go back and look at the notes I once deemed very clever then to realize they are the same words I sent a month before, and a month before that, the same again, and so on back to the beginning of online dating time. A conduit to look and see, that is all they are.

Whatever it was that I wrote, I formed the message in a way that persuaded Sara we should meet for breakfast. It snowed that morning, enough my car lost traction on the road more than once, and I wondered each time if what I was doing was worth it. I could slide in a ditch and never walk again, all so I could get somewhere to meet someone who may never want to see me again? I had barely started online dating and already it was draining my mind of the precious last bits of sense my parents once gave me.

Still I went. I veered through the iciness and parked my car on a street that had yet to be plowed then walked a block through the snow and stepped inside the homey restaurant. As I brushed off my coat, stomped my feet on the mat, I noticed a woman in a booth drinking coffee. She saw me too, but I couldn't be sure, so I asked the waitress, "I'm looking for a Sara?"

The waitress graciously understood, and I was led to the woman in the booth who had begun to smile, broadly, from her waist to the top of her head. It made her seem younger than the age she listed. She was ruddy, with her hair folded over to one side of her head.

"Snowy out there," I said as I sat down.

"Yeah," she said, holding back a smile I could tell had lit up rooms. "Definitely."

"Wanted to make sure I got the right person. Kinda new to this."

"Glad you made it." Her eyes were bright green. "I like your beard."

"Thanks," I said as I gave it a stroke. "I've actually been thinking I might shave it."

"No-no," she said, examining my face. "You should keep it. Keeps you warm, right?"

I agreed. And there in the diner, ensconced in red vinyl and Minneapolis memorabilia, Sara told me of the places she had lived. In Boston where the men were "short and angry." In Portland where she worked with a member of an all-girl punk group, popular in the late-90s and early 00s. Then in Sioux Falls, where we both had been. The occupational geography lesson took up most of breakfast and afterward, by her car, we had a short kiss goodbye. I think I tasted a flake of snow with her lip gloss.

The next time I brought a television show called *Deadwood* on DVD to her apartment. Once, that would have been too soon, but I had changed, or maybe eroded as I matured into my early thirties. When my years of online dating started, I thought of myself like Tiger Woods. In that man's whole life, he never understood women. But when he became the most dominant athlete in the world, he found it like breathing to have one. It was impossible to turn down, because every time it was offered, it struck him as novel. I don't have that much money or power or fame, but I felt the same. Like him, I was blown away with the thought of someone I hardly know wanting to be naked in front of me, wanting to kiss me in all the places I once dreamed of when the best I could do was look at a magazine and hope.

Tiger Woods didn't occupy my thoughts on the way to Sara's, who agreed to me coming over on the provision I was not, as she texted, a "creeper." I didn't think I was—though I had never heard the term—and drove to her place, to a marginal neighborhood I would not have expected a woman like Sara, someone in their mid-30s working in advertising, would live in. I parked behind her brick building, and as I walked toward her I could hear my footsteps on the quiet sidewalk in December. Hannah and I would meet in a little over a month.

We did not watch much of the show. Nude, in the glow of the title screen repeating, Sara told me about her old boyfriend. They had bought a car together, then he left her, sticking her with the bill for a gas-guzzling SUV. I do not know why she told me such personal things, though I didn't mind. The glow of the moon illuminated her body as she shifted on the couch. Her ample backside pushed into the cushions and she tapped her foot against me, checking to see if it would wake. We both looked down and smirked like an old couple. Past midnight, hardly knowing each other, it seemed a natural thing. I did not sleep over, though Sara did walk me to her door, and it excites me now, in a way a man can get excited, how she did that. It was the way she walked. I can see it now.

Our next time together, we watched *The Obscure Object of Desire*. And instead of the moon and street lights, we had her living room lamp. Lying across her old couch, surrounded by her, she finished, then she switched over to me and I released into her mouth. After, she went to her bathroom, and I could hear her spitting it out in the sink, which I found appealing, as if she could not handle everything I had. When she came back to the couch, we snaked our bodies together and watched the rest of the film in what I think must be this world's best imitation of heaven.

Sara came to my suburbs late at night a few days later, her makeup done, wearing a cotton dress, tights, and tall leather boots, as well as her coat with faux-fur lapels. Her broad, knowing smile was the most attractive thing she wore. She had an uncontrollable, lovely laughter, which I heard as I gave her the tour of the house: the kitchen without a table, a room where my landlord kept his junk, then the living room where I had my new prized possession, a big-screen TV. We watched a Timberwolves game.

"I don't know if I even like this," she said as I rubbed her leg, moving her tights. "It seems too real, or maybe like everything is fake?"

Soon, it did not matter. We were upstairs. I had a lamplight, not the fixture from directly above, all harsh and bright, and on the wall was one framed piece of art, a drawn recreation of a picture taken of me and my sisters in the early 90s. The rest of my meager possessions in my spartan attic were in neat order, so I was ashamed to put Sara down on a mattress—borrowed from my landlord—on the floor. This is where she did the things I loved. And I described them to my friend later—when he asked what she did because he liked to live vicariously through me as he was in a long-term relationship—and that's how the Ballsucker nickname began. I loved what she did. If I had not, I wouldn't have told him. After we dressed, Sara drove home in her SUV, back through the cold Minneapolis evening.

That weekend we went to breakfast, at the same place where I would meet Hannah. Sara met me in the lobby wearing her coat with the fur lapels and the kind of sunglasses that turn darker with the sun, bright that cold day. We got a booth and ate our breakfast.

"Every man loves it," she was telling me. I drank orange juice while she drank coffee. I told her I had never and did not have any real desire to either. "You just haven't done it yet," she said. "Every man acts likes it is his right." She took a small sip. "And this is every man."

"I'm serious," I said. "I don't want to all that much, really."

Sara smiled, in a way that was unbelieving. "If you had the chance, you'd be like every guy and say it's the 'best thing in the world.' Men are disgusting."

"Hey," I objected. "Women are, what with their breasts and legs and butts." Sara slapped my hand. Her eyes seemed glassy but happy. We held hands for a bit. Later, I paid for the meal.

On the way out of the restaurant, Sara's arm hooked in mine as her glasses turned dark. It gave her a more adult appearance, as if she were already past the time when I would have a young wife. Maybe that's why I stopped calling, which is maybe why she never did either. To be honest, all this time later, I have no idea.

"I don't know what it is," she said as we walked through the parked cars, leaning her head on my shoulder. "But you make me comfortable."

I do not think I said a word. At her SUV, we kissed goodbye. We did not see each other again.

CHAPTER SIX

Three memories rattle around in my brain. I should let my mind eat them, but I don't. I want to remember. It want to always have a record of a time when I thought myself important enough to casually throw away something valuable. These are the three things that one day I will wake up and have forgotten, without even trying to.

I never used it, and I don't know why not. Maybe I thought I wouldn't have known how? I never had before, but I don't think it would have needed much instruction. Hannah never incorporated it for herself, at least not when I was present. I just like to remember when she showed it to me. On some lazy afternoon in that pink bedroom of hers, with the mirrored closet sliding doors and wood floors, she pulled it out of a drawer and held the orange-colored phallus—complete with faux veins—and smiled a crooked smile.

Another thing: never in the time I knew Hannah was she late. Whatever is imbued into young girls to make them believe it is good to be tardy, so as to create a sense of desire, Hannah must have missed it. Because I would wait on her from time to time—when she would need to gather up her things or get ready—but being on time when I needed her, Hannah would never waver from that.

The last thing is on some hot afternoon, summers ago. We had been out at the lake, then come back to my place to recuperate in the coolness of the house. The shades were closed and we drank cold ciders. Hannah napped, her oval eyes closed, her heavy lips drooping to one side of her face. I turned on *Netflix*, only to come across a movie about nymphomaniac nuns. And actually, as far that kind of thing can go, it was well done. I went back to one of the same scenes twice, so again a nun spread open her dark robe—showing me the film was made in the late 80s—and as I watched the second time, I found myself getting excited. I looked over at Hannah and realized, when she woke, I would be with her. Perhaps, she dreams of me.

So I took off my shorts. And when Hannah groggily sat up and saw what I was doing, she gave me a look. It was one of disbelief, yes, like, what do you think you're doing with that thing? Though at the same time it was happiness, a funny kind of lovely happiness. She went to me without hesitation.

CHAPTER SEVEN

I work in the business of producing generic pharmaceuticals. As a Lead now, which means I watch over
things. I call maintenance when maintenance needs to
be called. I change the labeler when a roll of labels runs
out. I ensure the product mixes at the right speed. This
all amounts to very little. Though back in the time after
Sara, I was even less. Screwing caps on bottles, putting
instruction inserts into boxes of medicines, stacking full
cardboard boxes of medicine onto pallets.

Over three years ago now after doing just that, I went
home to the suburbs. First thing, to the kitchen to warm
something in the microwave, then straight upstairs to
check my messages. They were, sadly, the best part of
my day. Especially so that night, I thought I might have
another from FairDemoiselle.

Hot leftover pizza burning my mouth, my heart sank as I opened my email and saw nothing. But I couldn't help it, I decided to look at her profile anyway. The strange and modern advertisement, hers—and everyone else's—was meant to create something as abstract as love. FairDemoiselle's strategy was to keep her details to a minimum, mentioning that she wanted someone taller and she went to school part-time and worked part-time. Little else, other than a few lines in French.

For me, that was plenty. Her European outfits, her sandy blonde hair and emotional eyes, a certain *je ne sais quoi*. Even if she grew up near where I lived at the time, in the suburbs and not far from the oldest fully enclosed, climate-controlled mall in the United States, FairDemoiselle seemed to be from another world. Losing myself in our jet-setting future, she popped up online right as I poured over her pictures. And though it was considered a gauche thing to do, I started a conversation. She must have been accustomed to words suddenly appearing on her screen. Somehow, we began talking.

"You're not so bad yourself," I found myself somehow writing.

She had told me how attractive I was, and I think could have heard her say that forever. By two in the morning, we had begun to discuss what we wore to bed.

The subject of her backside came up, which she claimed to be something, and I imagined it the way a detective investigates a murder, with grave seriousness and the utmost attention to detail. What happened after that, I don't know how, but I was typing my address then she was telling me she would be right over. I looked at the clock on my computer. It was nearly three.

In the ten minutes it took FairDemoiselle to come over, I waited in the living room on the corduroy-upholstered red couch, trying not to wake my land-lord as I felt my prick get harder. When I heard a car park on the street, I sat up and saw her between the blinds, out beyond the hills of snow in the yard. FairDemoiselle stepped out of her wagon, all bundled up, then walked right up to the house, to the front door. She did it so confidently.

The lamp in the living room was our only light as FairDemoiselle, whose name was Brittany, unwrapped her scarf. We said hello. If she was disappointed or the awkward hug was just her way, I could not tell, but she said little, barely nodding when I asked if she wanted a tour of the living room and kitchen. I gave her the tour, since I did not know what else to do. After showing her the two or three rooms I could show, clicking the lights on then off again as we went, we came back to the living room. She took off the rest of her winter wear, resting it over the smaller loveseat with the same red corduroy upholstery.

"Do you want anything to drink?" I asked.

"No thanks," she said. "Should we go upstairs?"

"Yeah," I said, "sure." So we went, up to my attic with its carpeted floor and ceiling coming together in a steeple. Our plan had been to read from a novel.

"So here it is," I said as I handed it to her.

On my bed—her legs stretched out and her head resting against the wall—she examined the book written by a once obscure author, an alcoholic who spent time in mental hospitals and died alone in the south. This was one of his slimmer works, and it had struck me how it chronicled the lives of two sisters. FairDemoiselle, covered in tattoos, worked at an artisan pizza place but lived at home in the suburbs and went to school at Minneapolis Community and Technical College. She gave me a puzzled stare, as if she had just woken up from a drug-induced coma, and handed back the book. I did not know what else to do. I could only begin to read.

I have to say that it was strange, as if taking off her skirt and black lace tights and slapping her face as she swallowed me whole would have been less intrusive. Maybe that was what she wanted. I don't know. I just read.

When done, FairDemoiselle, Brittany, a woman of a million names, gave me a look a pet gives when it does not understand its master.

"That was good," she said. "You read well."

"Thanks. I mean, I can keep on reading if you like?"

"No," she said. "I'm tired. It's okay if I sleep here?"

"Of course," I said as I got up from my wooden chair. There was one chair and a round wooden table up in that attic as well, and I considered, for a moment, turning the lights down only slightly, strolling back over and taking her.

Instead, I turned them off, and in the darkness I undressed to my underwear. Then I lay down beside her, not close enough for our shoulders to touch. The moon gave some light, and we did not speak. Brittany stayed over the covers as I began to fear I was not the very interesting and attractive man she sought out. Her breathing was steady for what seemed like years. After a few minutes, it became more labored, so I moved closer. When it became like moaning, I began to softly kiss her, as slowly as could be. And the next thing I knew FairDemoiselle was on her knees as she grabbed a handful of it and asked, since we had talked about in length only an hour before, "Do you like it?"

And I did. A protruding righteous thing, not able to be contained by her red boyshorts. I kissed her there, sensing the ink up and down her legs. This moment will always be accompanied by equal measures of astonishment and blessing.

In the morning we kissed goodbye by the front door at my landlord's house in the suburbs. And I should have known, by the way she missed my lips, nodded her head and walked out into the cold without looking back, that I would not see her again. But I didn't. I really did not. That makes me a fool, I understand, but I don't care.

Only now do I begin to wonder how many hearts FairDemoiselle broke with her significant backside and disaffected air. I would warn the others she might message that she is not to be taken lightly. She does not consist of the same tissues as you, unknowing online dater.

I could tell them that, yes. Though if they are like me, what would it matter? They would not listen.

CHAPTER EIGHT

The night we had Thai. Or it could have been before that, when we had pancakes. Or before that, when we chatted online but had no long lines of laughter, only reserved reactions. If lucky, a singular "ha."

How stupid that sounds, how superficial of a reason it would be if that were why we could not be together. But how we ate pancakes was something we should have noticed. How we had to coax happiness out of many of our moments. How we had to make it seem as though we were having the best time, when we knew there were better times, with others better for us.

All of that is true, I think, there are people with that kind of love, those who are all day laughing and finishing each other's sentences. Why should I deserve that kind of thing? I was not born with it as a right. I am here to live and to die and to expect more is to be disappointed. I suppose that's why I'm here, disappointed. Still, Hannah was so pretty, and nice, what more is there? We went out for Thai food.

"You're going to love this," Hannah said as we stood in the restaurant's small lobby, waiting for a table. Around us were Buddhist figurines and peace flags, vases filled with sticks of incense, small elephantine statues.

"I bet I will," I said. "You're a good food recommender."

Hannah gave me a kiss on the forehead. I had always wanted to be that kind of couple, the kind who gives kisses to each other after everything. Though after my lips left her head, the din of the restaurant seemed deafening. We had nothing to say.

Thankfully, the hostess took us to our table. Nighttime in the city, where to our right was Franklin Street, the side of the street with the high-rise apartments close to the river where Somalis live. On the other side for blocks are old houses with twenty-somethings who garden and ride bikes and work in organic grocery stores. Right across the street is a liquor store. We ate vegetarian spring rolls.

"When we're done here," Hannah said, "let's get over and get *Strongbows*."

"That sounds good," I said. "I wonder what you're like when you're drunk."

"I get sleepy," Hannah said, then another silence. Desire lived in it, I think. Maybe even affection. But it was silence. There was always too much silence for us. We always ignored it.

I ordered what Hannah said to order, noodles with chicken and peanuts, while she got a tofu dish with co-conut sauce. She wore a red dress with white polka dots, while I wore a suit jacket and gray pants and dress shoes, and I hope, if someone noticed us from another table, they were jealous of the promise we seemed to hold. For that night at least, I hope so.

After our meal, we walked to the liquor store hold-ing hands. With our drinks in a brown paper bag, we went back to her place nearby. What happened after that, I don't know. If it hadn't happened, maybe it would have never happened. Maybe I would be with Hannah now. We would have a life together. She would be an art-ist, and me, a stay-at-home dad. We would have a child, perhaps two, name them Cecilia and Magnus. I could be Hannah's assistant.

We arrived to the house, a tall rental with two units. At the bottom, I later learned, lived a group of bearded men who sold weed. On the top was Hannah and other artists. We went up the aging wooden stairs, and as Hannah opened the door I was greeted by the kitschy furnishings: the walls of misshapen rock, couches that had seen God only knew, a fish tank with no fish inside but some kind of sculpture. Singing came from the kitchen, but the singer did not hear us enter. Not until we got very close did she notice us, and when she did, she jumped. She even screamed in surprise, then she turned, and I saw her. After seeing her face, I heard her laugh. Since hearing it, I have not heard another as good.

"Oh my god," she said, her presence piercing my gut. "You guys scared me." She wore feather earrings and had a pert face, like she came from a Belle and Sebastian album cover.

"Sorry about that," Hannah said as they hugged. They both looked at me. "Daniela, this is Robert."

"So nice to meet you." She brushed off her hand to shake mine. "Sorry about the mess. I'm making bread." What else would an angel be doing on a Friday than something wholesome like baking?

"Robert and I were just going to go up and watch a movie." Hannah seemed to want to hold my hand, but

I wanted to cut it off if it meant someone other than Daniela was holding it. I had known her for perhaps a minute.

"A movie and *Strongbows* sounds wonderful," Daniela said, turning to the oven to attend to the bread. That's when I saw it, and she was so round there, it seemed like a ribald cartoonist drew her. I had to look away. I put the leftovers in the fridge and held onto the ciders.

"Nice meeting you, Daniela," I said. "Good luck in the bread opera." And though it was not that funny, Daniela's laugh filled every space of the kitchen. Its echoes went up the winding stairs, lingering as Hannah showed me the nook with blankets and pillows where guests stayed in the hall and the rest of the one-of-a-kind prints on the cracking walls. Lastly, there was Daniela's room.

"That's hers at the end," Hannah said as she opened the door of her room. "It was pained pink before we moved in...so I knew it had to be mine."

I looked, and thoughts of Daniela faded. Hannah's walls were so pink, and everything else was so colorful: the yellow comforter on her bed, a crayon-colored print of a strange carnival, trinkets in every hue of the rainbow on her bookshelf. To the left, her closet sliding doors and the full body mirrors.

"What do you think, Mr. Robert?" she asked, and I took her in my arms to forget.

"It's perfect," I said. We stripped off our clothes. Hannah's backside was to the mirror. I gave it a small slap, and she responded by caressing the top of my head. We moved to her bed.

The colors of room obfuscated by the dark night, and Hannah breathed out. She seemed relieved. "Now where did that come from?"

I smiled as she rested on my chest, like she did before we separated to our sides. Hannah was happy for me and I was at least glad I did not have to explain myself, that my actions were enough. Still, it may have been just as well I never improved in bed with Hannah. Because the thing that made me useful—even in the silent moments after—was the creation connected to the one downstairs making bread, the one who laughed as if she knew every joy in the world.

CHAPTER NINE

There was someone before Hannah who almost veered me off this course and into a life of content, adult singleness. I can see the future she almost set in motion, one in which I take down my profile and stop online dating, and instead I funnel my energy into creating, maybe furniture or leather goods. If I were not so stubborn, this would have happened. If I were just a bit smarter, I know it would have.

In this alternate dimension I realize how fruitless trying is, and instead of searching I focus on my career, so now I am in charge of an entire side of the factory, as I know I would have never made any leather goods. The bosses are no world beaters. They are older, yes, they do have that. But they are facile, inept and slow.

All it would've taken is someone with a little more focus and get up, along with a few more connections, which I could have been fostering had I not been drowning in the throes of crush after senseless crush.

Who knows, if I had deleted my profile after her, I might now be making enough money that I would not be worrying about any of this. I would not care about return calls from someone I barely know, wondering how, exactly, I should craft a message to make myself seem interested in but also oblivious to her affection. I would not worry about what I should write to a stranger so as to appear manly yet sensitive. All that, I could have left behind, given it up to younger men with fire in their bellies, concrete coursing through their cocks. They have hearts as pliable as hot copper. Instead here I am, older and grayer, less hearty, still at it.

Her name was Tara. Pronounced TAR-ah, as she would point out to me, she was the one for whom I sent maybe one of my best first messages. I've sent countless by now, but hers was one of my bold ones, detailing how we would one day be telling our children how strange it was we met online. I was drunk, I think, when I wrote it, so it may not have seemed too over the top to me at the time. Indeed I must have been drunk because it was not until Tara wrote back a week or so later, at the beginning of December, when I remembered the gin from that night. Her message applauded me on my bravado and prompted me to look once more.

Tara, from her profile, looked to be a developed woman working on her Ph.D. in, as I would later learn, comparative literature. She had appealing dark features, though she wrote in her profile that she did not want anyone messaging her if they had a "fetish for Middle Eastern women." And even though she tried to hide them with winter coats and prearranged angles, she had breasts which, I imagine, would have taken two full hands to hold just one. She was short, and I would appreciate how short—her unruly bosom made it all the more apparent—when I met her.

The morning of our date, I did what I do every morning. Look up other jobs. Dream of a different life. On rare mornings I read. Every so often, I have a date. And as I sat alone, an hour before leaving, Tara's avatar blinked up on my computer screen.

"Robert," her words read, "good morning. I'm sorry but..." She went on to tell me about how she felt under the weather, offering that we "perhaps soon reschedule." I agreed, but with a thud of hollowness. I wanted to show Tara how strong I could be.

I wanted to tell her something brazen and ballsy like, "You missed out, baby, this was your one chance." Instead, I sent a message to her about the next time we could see each other. I heard nothing in response.

The holidays came and went. When I got back to the suburbs, I asked my landlord to take new pictures of me for the dating website. I had purchased an ensemble with Christmas money from my parents. Pale gray slacks, dress shoes, tweed suit jacket, a white dress shirt, and a blue tie with patterned white dots. And though I had no job which required a suit, or any pursuits which necessitated one, I believed pictures in one might enhance my chances. So that's we did, my landlord and I, we had a fashion photo shoot around the house. He kept saying what we were doing was ridiculous, but these are the pictures that led me to Hannah. They are the ones that gave me the confidence to send one last message to Tara.

She must have been surprised when she saw them. I probably looked undateable to her in the other pictures: fatter, less ambitious, maybe even drunk. Not a day after my message—ending with "so sad you missed out… " — she clicked on my profile several times, all in the same day, and that means everything in that world, and soon we had a date.

At nearly the same time as the last, at a coffee shop near her house, I parked my car nearby and walked out into a suffocating cold. Hustling inside, I sat down at a table as light streamed in through glass doors of the bean-roasted place. Minutes later, I received a text.

"Running a late. Be there soon!" And Tara was right, she got there in the exact amount of time I would call soon, apologizing as we stood in a short line to get coffee.

"I am so sorry," Tara was saying. "I was helping my roommate with a paper. We're more than roommates, friends, really. Best friends, maybe. I don't know, she looks up to me, and it was on 19th Century French novelists and I love helping her because she's so sweet. Oh God, I'm babbling. Sorry. And sorry, again, for being late."

I did not want her to stop babbling. Maybe ever. I thought about how much - the way she talked, her presence, all the down to her posture - seemed like how I imagined it would be when I met my wife.

We drank our coffee and discussed Woody Allen films—she said "anything from the late 70s/early 80s is gold"—along with her work in comparative literature, as well as the people behind us who we hypothesized were on their first date. At one point, I became bold enough to brush Tara's fingers—though we knew it was on purpose—as she held her coffee cup. She took my hand in response. I took her home—she walked there in the cold—and we kissed goodbye in my car for a while. I watched her get out and go to her brick apartment building. As she unlocked her glass front door, she looked back. She blew a kiss.

Later that day, Tara texted to say she would not be able to get together until the next week. We had waited 30 years for each other; we would have to wait another week? I would have to be patient. Even if I did not think I would make it, the evening of our movie marathon, which we planned in detail over the week, did arrive. I was at a large, round table alone at break time as the rest of the workers ate their lunch—lots of dehydrated packaged sandwiches from the vending machine—and we watched the news.

Its comforting buzz played in the background as I enveloped myself in the messages Tara had sent. I was thinking of her face and her laugh, the possibility of her breasts, when her voicemail appeared. Phone reception at work is awful, so this will happen from time to time. A message will be delayed by the dense fog that must cover our building. I went outside and listened.

"...And I don't want you to think I'm a flake," I barely heard. "Because I'm really not, but tonight is not going to work. I have too much reading. By tomorrow night, I think, things should be calmed down, so let's do that..."

"Tomorrow would be fine," I typed. I could reply with nothing else.

The next day at the same table at almost the exact same time as the same story played on the news, I had another message. This time she sent a text.

"I'm sorry, but something's come up. Please don't think I don't want to hang out because I do. How about Tuesday, and Saturday? I should be free both days."

Tara, pronounced TAR-ah, a dark-featured woman born in Canada with parents from Iran who knew about the world and was perfect, I could not give up on her. So I went out again, and this time I called. She answered right away.

"Hey, everything ok? Did something 'suddenly come up?'" I wondered if she got *The Brady Bunch* reference.

"Robert, I'm sorry, but, okay, let me just ask this before anything else. Is it weird to come over at night to watch movies for a second date? We're just going to watch movies, right?"

"Yeah, I thought that's what we were doing. Woody Allen, right?"

"Right, and I want to, I just don't think it's the best idea, you know, for a second date. What are you doing Saturday? Why don't we go get pho?"

We had talked about pho. Though as I stood outside watching my breath dissipate, I saw in my mind the movies growing cold in my car. I saw myself bringing them inside to the attic in the suburbs with the GPS I would not use to make sure I would make it to her place on time.

"Sure," I said. "Pho's good. I mean, we can do pho."

"Great. Let's do that. Okay, I should go, Robert. I'll see you soon."

"Okay. Bye, Tara." But she had already hung up.

We did meet that weekend, but it was only our flesh. Someone had replaced everything else. As Tara came upon the booth, the look she gave me seemed confused, as if she was meant to meet someone else. She wore glasses that day, black thick-framed ones, as I had told her I liked the picture where she wore them. With that small victory, we tried to fight back. But her heels dragged behind us, creating two lines. The lines became a trail. The trail became a ditch as we ate, and I found myself gazing off at a table of young people, tattooed and nose-ringed and boisterous. If Tara and I looked that happy at coffee, I don't know. It's just how I imagined we looked.

After that we were relegated to the internet, just chatting, and that is when the topic of sex surfaced. I tried to ask who he was—a boyfriend or no, if he lived in town—but Tara would not say, only throwing out that she had someone else on occasion and let it float like a bobber I could not reach. Not long after that, she sent the email, the one that ended with, "I really am sorry. It's just, I'm too busy for anything at the moment."

My wife had found another lover; that's how it felt. Such a drastic way to react, I know, though it seemed right, which says too much about me. I replied to say I was thankful for the email, even though there is no way I ever could be.

"I have lots of questions," I wrote. And I did, about her other, about our coffee, and what she thought of me. "But those questions aren't meant for us. I liked being around you. You're someone I didn't anticipate meeting on that site, someone with whom it feels right."

"Well," she wrote in response that afternoon. "We can talk about your questions if you want. But not right at this moment, because I have to go eat."

And that was it. She left in a haze, one I started to come out of when I met Hannah, though I never fully did, to be honest, as the memory of Tara lingers. To be completely bare, my only comfort came recently, as I will, on occasion, go to her online profiles. No, it is not healthy, but we all do unhealthy things.

"Making salad and frozen pizza with the boyfriend," Tara posted. "Sometimes you just have to do it."

And at first that devastated me, though soon after—loping around the house in the suburbs, scrounging for food to numb my mind—I became washed with a comfort. The cleansing I gathered from those words went like this: I don't know how well Tara gets along with that man, if he creates in her "nervous heart bubbles," as she posted the afternoon of our coffee date. I don't know if he is the kind of man she wakes up next to and is glad to jump out of bed—or stay in it—because he is near. I don't know, but the thing that calmed my heart and pushed it away from the bruising pain Tara can bring when I let her enter my mind, is that whoever he is, however much she thinks of him, I know where they met.

So no matter how long Tara is with him, no matter much love they accrue, in the end, she will never be able to take back the fact that once, long ago, she met her husband in a place she has always been ashamed to reveal. Unless they met in real life and not through the dating website. In that case, I hope I never think of her again.

CHAPTER TEN

We had our pancakes and our Thai and Hannah began coming over to the suburbs when I was not home yet from the factory. She had told me about the Jewish boy and her Indian man, and about a man in Florida—who lived near her mom—who she slept with on occasion but no longer would. Our profiles had been cut down to bare bones. We were more or less together.

In that time, Hannah's SUV would be parked on the street before I got home, and she would be inside with something healthy for me to eat – she made tomato basil mozzarella sandwiches on French bread – and later, after watching TV and drinking wine, we would be together. Still I continued to search. I found another.

KatyRed was her profile name, with professional photos, as if taken in a studio. We ate soup on the same Sunday afternoon I texted Hannah to say I would not be able to come over because of the weather. I instead went to see a woman, a girl really, with sideswiped reddish hair and big eyes and even bigger lips. She would be the one to understand me so well I would only later chuckle at the times when I was an online dater.

Her perfection, I did my best to convince myself of it as I stood in front of a bathroom mirror in the suburbs. My landlord was in the living room playing online games, oblivious to any consternation as I silently berated myself for being a coward, allowing nature to best me in my search for happiness. I had to go through all this to find true love, so I gave myself a shake of the head and went upstairs to my attic to get dressed.

In my winter wear, I went outside where it took a good ten minutes to clear away the snow from my car. It took more to shovel enough down the driveway so I could even hope to reverse out onto the road. The bottom of my jeans wet, windows melting the new flakes coming down, I punched the gas and went backward. Fishtailing out, I wound my car down the side streets, powdered with untouched inches. It seemed no one else in the suburbs had plans of going anywhere, though as I drove I became resolved. I congratulated myself for being so brave.

After arriving early, as I always do, I looked out through the windows of the restaurant. More snow came down. It seemed so peaceful when not driving in it. Soon Katy was in front of me, and immediately I knew she was not the one. From the first words she said, it was clear she would never fill me with the feeling Tara, pronounced TAR-ah, imparted. Still we had a time. Katy was attractive, and I needed to continue to forget I had arranged this date.

She lived nearby and invited me over afterward to smoke in her Uptown apartment. There, crossed legged across from me beside her tiny TV, she gave me a view of her. Her underwear was white, with little red hearts. I rubbed my socked feet against her thighs. We did what we did

At her door, I asked for her number, and she wrote it down on a small ripped off piece of newspaper—one I still have—then we kissed sloppily as our goodbye. Before I knew it, her door was closed, and I walked to my car in the snow that still came down. I had driven through hell to meet a stranger, and all the while I had someone good. As I marveled at the cars stuck on the interstate, I swore I would never stray again.

Even as I said that, I held the last embers of something else. SongsBeingSun, from her main profile picture where she held a sock puppet, to another where she stretched her muscled brown back in a yellow summer dress, seemed to be someone who went on few dates with men from the internet. She could fill her life with art and be happy. A seriousness flowed through our messages where we planned to perform a play that would skewer online dating. I would write it and she would stage it all with her homemade puppets. It took time, but eventually, SongsBeingSun, or Mona, a striking woman with parents from Bolivia, gave me her number. By the time she did, I was with Hannah. My pact made in a blizzard was bonded and sealed.

So Mona's number lived in my phone for months, and every so often I would dial it, pushing the number nearer the top. I would even consider letting the phone ring more than once, though I never did. At some point, I stopped entirely, until her number fell through the bottom of my history and into oblivion.

But still to this day I can see Mona looking in her mirror. She wears a green and pink checkered dress, and the mirror reflects her flawless skin and symmetrical lips, and bangs, such bangs. She has the kind of face I would fall in love with; a face, if I had known, I would've broken my weak contract for.

How easily I would've broken it. I was never a saint. And in the times I might have been, it's only because I had no opportunities to be a sinner.

CHAPTER ELEVEN

For two years after college I was in love with someone who did not love me. We worked at a group home in Nebraska. It was an unrequited thing that does not bear repeating other than to say I spent a year or so praying for something hopeless, and after that another year slowly moving to the knowledge that it was. When those spans of time ended, my twenties were half gone.

Lost time propelled me to the Pacific Northwest where I desired to be with as many undressed women who would say my name as loudly as I could inspire. When that ended, I moved to Minneapolis and went online to find a partnership, not a supplication, like in my youth, or a tryst, like after that. Hannah was neither. She was everything I could have ever wanted.

By the afternoon of Hannah at the puppet theater, I could be a man. I could support my partner's endeavors. To get ready, I ironed my suit. We would be declaring our partnership to the world. I would need to be dressed as handsomely as I could be dressed. With my clothes crisp, beard trimmed, face fresh with aftershave, I drove through the cold. The streets white, the snow jagged as sheets of glass, but the sun was gracious. She shined her light as I drove to get Hannah an arrangement of flowers.

Before that day, flowers had always been, for me, the sign of a last-ditch effort to save something already lost. They would be different that day. The green plant with white petals foreshadowed goodness as I traveled north to the city for Hannah's art show.

Art show is maybe not what it should be called. All I know is what I saw. As one of the first there, I could pick any seat. In that small theater, there was room for maybe fifty people, enough for a few friends and artistic moms and dads and their long-haired children. I sat against the wall, behind the first two rows where a group of college students loudly whispered to each other. I thumbed through the program, proud to know a featured artist.

The curtains opened, and first up was a man and a woman whose puppet show included a troll who kept cutting down trees, and in the end very bad things happened to him. They were adorable, those hippies, and when they took their bow, the man in his fearsome beard showed off a goofy smile and grimy teeth which must have not seen a dentist since grade school. His partner was just as endearing, with a body, curving well from earthy drugs not synthetic supplements. She had long, straight brown hair and wore a sarong skirt and a tight shirt. She was beautiful, but I was not jealous. I was glad for them, for their lives as traveling puppeteers. I was with Hannah.

A man came up after that with a life-sized puppet that looked amazingly real. So much so it seemed jarring when at the end the two had an honest to goodness wrestling match. After that was a bit of Disney fare, with a piece involving a water tank, and I could have sworn the people behind tank had figured out a way to puppeteer from inside the water. Their prehistoric neon fish flitted and floated to spacey music. I enjoyed it all but was getting restless. I wanted to see Hannah.

Finally, the emcee introduced her. The curtains parted and two puppeteers emerged. Both dressed in black, one in charge of a small crate with wooden legs and red shoes. He danced his puppet, evading balls lobbed haphazardly from the other puppet, a larger but same crate-bodied creature. The smaller one scampered off the stage and came back out as a slightly larger pair of wooden legs with red shoes, but the same thing happened, the still larger crate won. This game repeated itself until a second curtain pulled back to reveal giant wooden legs and red shoes, all maneuvered by Hannah. Then down on the bully crate came a cascade of plastic balls—which she told me she bought after an *Arby's* Playland shut down—and out into the audience.

The children—who all seemed to love Hannah's show—ran around and threw the balls back on stage. After everything was picked up, with what was left of the audience, the puppeteers fielded questions. The college students from the front row asked the most, as I watched Hannah, who sat at the end with her legs crossed. Before that day, I had known heartache and times of being unlucky. It seemed the universe was evening things out. Hannah peered up at me, smirking. I did not think of Tara or the numbers in my phone or some mystical person. I knew the miracle of knowing someone was thinking of me.

I headed down to her when the questions ended. Unable to contain my happiness, I must have been beaming, though as Hannah approached, she seemed to crumble. She turned down her head, resting it on my suit.

"Oh Robbies, it was bad," she said, muffled by my body, "wasn't it?"

"Bad?" I kissed her hair. "What are you talking about?"

"The balls didn't fall, Robbie, didn't you notice? See, they're stuck up there." And she lifted her head and pointed at the lodged group.

"I thought it was great, Hannah. Really." Taking her shoulders, I kissed her on the lips. "I'm glad I could see this." And I was. I was grateful.

Hannah seemed to believe me, brightened back to her usual self quickly, and went to gather her things. I watched the hippies in their ragged coats leave, carrying with them a tuba, their puppets and an easel. I wondered they where they would stay. I hoped they found somewhere warm. The dark theater was mostly empty as Hannah and I left into the bright day, shielding our eyes, holding hands.

At her house I gathered up the flowers from my passenger seat. The day had turned grayer, so it was cloudy as we approached one another. I put the flowers behind my back, but Hannah spotted them and was not surprised.

"These are for you," I said as I revealed them.

"Daises," she said. "I thought you might bring me daisies." She smelled them. "I told Daniela you would."

"I thought they might be appropriate."

"They're nice, Robbies, thank you." We were holding hands as we went up to put them in water.

Hannah went up to change into other clothes and I waited in the living room. After maybe a minute, it hit me. Why was I not with my baby? So I jumped up, though just as I got in the kitchen, I ran into her on the way down.

"I was just on my way up," I said.

"Were you?" she said, touching me. "What were you going to do?" And we came together, right there on the table. When it was done, she led me to my car.

"Also," she said as went down the stairs, "you'll be getting more action later."

I felt such grace, though even on our what is our best day, I believe, as I lay beside Hannah that night after hearing her completely finish and she slept with small endearing snorts, I could not sleep myself. A dread crept up my throat. I did not want to be there. There was another bed somewhere else I needed to be in, with someone else I did not yet know.

CHAPTER TWELVE

My first after Hannah started humbly. LindseyRunning, Lindsey in real life, and I went out for a meager bowl of soup. I could never do six dollar drinks, then seven dollar clam appetizers, then eight dollar calamari, and on top of that a ten dollar movie, then more drinks—more expensive than the last—without hearing the hounding vacuum suction of a draining bank account.

The man does not need to pay, but would it be better if the woman did? Once we arrive at the answer, we realize, by our evolution, the man is the one who pays, as the woman is expected to maintain her body hair, and I don't see why that's a necessary thing. It's what we do, and until we evolve, it's what we will always do.

Some say eating dinner on a first date, even for something as simple as soup, is the worst thing. One must order, wait, get the bill. But the idea that alcohol is mandatory to be interested or interesting is something I cannot accept. No matter how long I live, how unattractive I grow or lonely I become, I hope being drunk is not the only way someone will want be with me. That day may come, I understand, but now it is an amplifier. All these first dates happening with all the drinks distracting those daters from how alone they are is too much. I cannot think of it. To drown those thoughts with alcohol makes things worse.

So I met Lindsey for pho, and the text came as soon as I sat down, "Running a couple minutes behind. Be there soon!"

For almost a year before I had been with Hannah. For almost a year I had known just her. No part of me mourned her absence. As if I were burning a book I had just written, not holding the words inside dear. I think, maybe, it was the cockiness of breaking up with someone. As I waited for Lindsey, I may have looked confident. That week, I had started a new position, beginning to make several more dollars an hour, and soon enough I would receive another promotion and my dollars an hour would raise again. Then it would no longer be soup, but drinks and clams and expensive public radio variety shows and all the rest.

Lindsey was across me: tall, with red hair, looking the part of a cross country runner on her way to becoming a woman. She may have gained the good weight in her backside working as a nanny, which she told me she did in Minneapolis as she prepared to take her LSATs. I ate, lucky for Lindsey be my first after Hannah. Lindsey wore lip gloss and talked through her nose, in a way charmingly, about what she had been doing for the last year in Oakland, working with Lutheran Volunteer Service.

"This is really tasty, Robert," she said, broth steaming her wire-framed glasses, her pale face. "Glad you thought of it."

"I am too," I said, and I even winked. I never wink.

After I finished I shoved my bowl to the side and sat with my back to the wall. My legs down my booth, we began to talk movies. "There's the theater by my house," I offered. "We could see what's playing there?"

"By your house?" she said, knocking my knee. "Why would we want to go there?"

"Well, in case we wanted to get a drink or something. I mean, we could go to your place?"

"No way, my place is a mess. Let's go to yours." So Lindsey and I left, walking close enough to bump into one other. I could smell her perfume. Its sweetness faded under the sickly streetlight where I gave her my address. She followed me home.

In the suburbs, Lindsey drank a vodka tonic as I gave the tour. In the living room, my landlord was playing his online games, and though he was my landlord and I was his tenant, I was superior. On the couch, Lindsey rubbing my head and drinking a drink, he had only his computer. And as he explained what he played, I admired Lindsey's shape, and her smell, clean laundry and perfume. I was enamored with her thighs as I squeezed them, firm but womanly.

Later, upstairs, and her stomach was like the meniscus of a cup of water. Her breasts were small but her nipples were thimbles, and I engulfed them. The condom was next. Linsey waited in bed, swimming her legs. As we reached my end, she shouted, "Fuck me, Rob, fuck me harder." And that's when it must have happened. I would have stopped had I known. I would've readjusted.

"What a second," she said, stopping her motion in a frustrated halt, pushing back her red hair. "Did you just come?

"Yeah." I rested my head on her shoulder. "I did."

"But you had a condom on, right? Why is it all over me?" She wiped herself by her shaved crotch.

"I don't know, I." I was stammering, but there it rested, greasy and uneasy, on my thigh. I picked it up. "It's here. It's fine."

"Are you sure?"

"It's not like I came in you," I said as I tossed it in on my underwear. "You would've felt that." But Lindsey did not laugh. She did stay the night, though it was a fitful sleep for us both.

In the morning we had a tender goodbye, as if we forgot everything, and the very next night Lindsey came over, more done up than on our first date. We had no premise. We went upstairs and Lindsey lay beside me in bed, fully clothed.

"It just has me a little weirded out," she said. "You understand, right?"

"Lindsey, really, there's nothing to worry about." I was only pretty sure of that, though I did my best to convey total certainty.

"I know," she said. "But maybe just right now." She sat up and said, "I don't know."

"You don't know?" I sat up too, kissed her on the cheek. She wiped it off.

"Maybe we should let things cool off."

I hardly put up a fight. Finding another seemed like breathing then. I did not worry as Lindsey stepped out of the house and into the suburbs after midnight. It must have been my aloofness bringing us to the *Cheesecake Factory* less than a week later. We held hands across the table in the cavernous place. Our menus thick as novels, Lindsey flipped through the laminated pages as I thought of her body, the one I dream of, the bottom-heavy, top-light thing I yearn for. She wore makeup that night, and she had a good face without any extra layers. Her face was plain and wonderful and only worsened by powders and lacquer, altering into something it was not.

"I'm sorry about the other day," she told me, a large salad in front of her. I had a hamburger and fries. "Honestly I was freaked out about that first night. But I feel better about it now. A lot." She kissed my hand, then took a bite.

We made love in the suburbs that night, "fucked," I suppose is a better way of saying it, and it is good to remember Lindsey's pale body. Though it is just as painful to remember this: no matter how long I could sustain myself, take her in every way I knew, whenever we were done she would not lie on my mattress in exhausted bliss, replete with sweat dripping from her brow. Instead she seemed undone, wanting more than what she had been given, asking if I could "go again." Never could I manage to.

Around that time, we had a picnic in a park near my landlord's house in the suburbs. I brought strawberries, cheese, wine, salami, and slices of bread and crackers. We sat under a lone tree in the middle of a park, with a pond nearby. Never did I feel too old with Lindsey, but that day she told me about showering with her entire college cross country team. I tried to hide my shock, taking a big drink of wine.

"It was like at the end of the year," she said. "Everyone is drunk. It really isn't a big deal. Like, it's never an orgy, if that's what you're thinking."

It was. I imagined the runners lathering each other, how the women snickered and the men leered at what had managed to grow on the opposite sex despite all the exercise.

"None of the guys had boners?" I must have seemed square to Lindsey. Balding, a worker at a job, disconnected from young, fun, sweaty things.

"No." Lindsey popped a strawberry in her mouth. "I don't think so. Like I said, it was just for fun. It wasn't like anybody was fucking each other in there. Just fun."

"I'm sure," I said. "I'm sure it was." And that brought a smirk to Lindsey's face. We even made out in the grass, making that day the best day for us. I don't think Lindsey—wherever she might be—or I, where I am, could point to another and say it was better.

For another month after the picnic we were together. We drank mixed drinks on the couch in the suburbs as we watched a detective show set in Baltimore, one Lindsey said I "had to watch," and in between episodes she'd get restless and want to talk about us—something I appreciate now—and after our talk in circles we'd go upstairs and I would kiss her, the only way I knew how, and she would wipe it off, then I'd take her on the mattress, the only way I knew how, and after it was done she would poke at me until she grew tired. Eventually, we would sleep.

Lindsey left me, or I may have left her. But even if I did, I soon missed her athletic form, her thimbles and convex stomach. I called because I had her muffin pan. We once made muffins. I had a reason to reach out to her.

Showered, shaved, I brought the pan upstairs to hint at where we should go. But she came in house in the suburbs that night without knocking, so I had to jump up to greet her in the kitchen. I saw there in high leather boots over tight jeans, and for the first time Lindsey seemed to have cleavage.

"Do you have it?" she asked.

"You look good," I said. "Going to your see your guy?"

"I should just get it and get going, Robert."

"Right," I said. "Right." Though even as I went up the stairs, I hoped Lindsey would follow. I even waited for a minute up there, but she never came. Back downstairs, she was already outside.

"Thanks," she said as she took it, and her next motion was a hop down the three cement steps. Not a moment lingered between us.

CHAPTER THIRTEEN

We were on the couch in the suburbs after my factory job a month or so before Hannah and the other five candidates in her program displayed their final work at a gallery. Hannah gave me a playful jab.

"You don't have to be there the whole time," she said.

I turned the channel to avoid her gaze. "You know they're sticklers about getting time off. I'll see what I can do." And somehow that was enough. She snuggled closer.

In the weeks after, Hannah would ask, in her way gently and sweetly, if I could come. Her family would be there, her divorced parents in Florida and Pennsylvania, her sister in New York. They would fly thousands of miles. I could drive less than twenty to see her work from the years when we did not know each other, but now, blessed to have met, could celebrate.

We had our routine then. During the day Hannah worked on her art, maybe programming a cartoon tree to talk or painting a colorful sky. In the afternoon she worked in the university's wood shop, routing commissioned projects or helping undergraduates with theirs. On some weekday nights, she taught a survey course on drawing. She was busy, but not too busy she could not see me.

Back in the suburbs, after my shift, Hannah would be there waiting for me while I drove home listening to Christian talk radio. Hearing it meant going away from work at the drug factory and the people who resented their life. A peace would wash over me as I heard the same man from a church in Seattle spew about how our president was leading our country in the wrong direction and why no one should ever use birth control. I loved hearing him.

But the best part of the drive came at the end. That house in the suburbs lived at the bottom of a small hill, so I would not see her car until I came over a rise. Going down the descent, first was the top half of her white

SUV, then my headlights shining on the fading outline of stickers for a children's television show in her rear window. Her car empty, I knew Hannah would be inside. We would watch a show on *The Food Network* that turned bad restaurants into good ones. We would drink wine. We would be with each other then fall asleep.

Her final thesis show approached, still the day before, the very night before, she asked me in bed, "Maybe you could get off for an hour or two?"

"I'll try," is all I said. But I did not. I watched small bottles of medicine on a conveyor go by as she had the biggest night of her life. Days later, my regret bloomed.

"It was a jerk thing to do," I said. We were out at dinner at the same Thai place we first went. "I should've been there. I would have loved to have seen it."

And it was true, I would have been proud to be by her side. Hannah in one the dresses that showed off her breasts, me in my suit, I could have soaked up residual adulation from those in the art scene. But that desire was weak compared to a knowledge; I could not be introduced as her man, not to her mom, her dad or her sister. Because then, whatever Hannah and I had left—a month, a year—when it ended, those in her family would have a face to connect with the name Hannah hated to repeat.

Soon after her thesis showing, I traveled to Chicago where I visited my friend for his birthday. And though Hannah said nothing about it, nor did I, we both must have internally noticed how I was able to get time off of work. Just weeks after that, Hannah wanted me to go to New York City with her to pick up her sister's car, as Hannah's SUV had broken down.

"It'll be a lot of fun, Robbies," she said. We were in the suburbs on my mattress, just past midnight. "I'll show you all the cool hipster spots." Hannah had tattoos, a pair of fuzzy dice behind her left ear, and on her left hip descending downward was an ice cream sundae with a cherry and a banana split, all swirling around.

I never asked for the time off work, and a stale month later, I drove to Hannah's place. Just after midnight again, the suburbs deserted, I was doing the right thing. Our futures I kept in mind. After that night, Hannah would be free to find someone who would kiss her as passionately as she desired. Take her to the new restaurants and bars around the city that I never did. And I could find my, whoever she was, the one who knew me so well I would never speak again. Reborn, I drove north.

At Hannah's street I got out of my car, and as I walked up to her place one last time I fished in my pockets for my phone, only to realize I'd forgotten it. I couldn't get in, unless I began yelling up to Hannah's room. I considered that for a minute or two until a band of cyclists rode up.

It was the downstairs tenants, the bearded drug dealers, two of them wearing parkas. They were kind enough to let me in, and I saw on their living room coffee table a vase half full of drugs, then in the kitchen there were beer boxes stacked higher than the refrigerator. I left their hedonistic life through a back door and went up the next set of stairs with good intentions.

Knocking gently, pushing the door open, Hannah was in her pajama pants. Her face freshly washed and computer on her bedspread, I sat on the bed, not so close that we could touch. She smiled weakly, as if she knew why I was there.

"Have you been to your neighbor's place?" I said, trying to add levity. "Holy moly, they have *a lot* of weed."

Hannah asked why I was there, quietly, and that's when I began. I didn't explain anything specifically and so she asked me for them. It's what we all want, I think. I thought she deserved them.

"Hannah, you're smart and pretty and obviously talented," I said. "I care for you a lot, it's just, okay, I guess if I'm being honest it does seem like you never laugh, you know. You never laugh at anything I say."

"God, why does every guy say that? Every guy." Hannah held her legs to her body, her knees touching her chin.

"Sorry, no, forget that, that doesn't matter. I want you to be happy, Hannah, and it seems like I don't make you as happy, not like you could be." She sat on her bed, facing that closet with the mirrors.

"I want to hold you, Robbies," she said, and they were so fragile, her words, they made me less than a worm, so I said the thing I would regret. Not only that night, but later when I would hear more or less the same words from others and remember how I once said, "Just, let's wait a bit and see how we feel after a few days."

Hannah was always gracious, so she said it for me, "Okay, I'll walk you out."

Several steps up above me at the bottom of her stairs, I saw Hannah in the outfit she must have worn for bed when I wasn't around—blue and yellow and soft, like a toddler's pajamas. She gave me a smile, the one she gave when I showed up for pancakes in the snow, the one I always saw whenever I made a joke, and the one, at that moment, was meant to be that way, unsure and about to crumble. I tried to look back in a way that showed how much I appreciated her, but I know that didn't come across. The door closed behind me.

That weekend, I could not stop thinking about Hannah. Maybe, if we started over, it would be different. So I called her on a Sunday night and begged for us to have brunch, and we did. We went to a hippie breakfast place in Seward Park, and by the end I was in Hannah's new smartphone. By that evening, she fell asleep on my chest.

Because of that there is one more place, her uncle's house vacation house in Delaware. Hannah asked me to go there after we got back together. We would have gone yachting, eaten lobster, done any number of other bourgeois activities. Again, though, I said I could not. If I had said yes, who knows, maybe I could have been a Kennedy, such a man with a first-class seat, enjoying five-star meals and idyllic views through ostentatious bay windows.

But I saw another breaking in our future, and going would have made that time worse. I would have already met a wealthy member of her family. So maybe one day I would have woken up with my knees broken or my bank account drained. I should consider myself lucky. Lucky, that must be what I am.

CHAPTER FOURTEEN

A s I look at myself now, I find it hard to believe the things that Julia—julesnotverne on the website— once did to my body. Years ago when I met her those things didn't seem so crazy. I could have been tight enough. In that time, I don't think I as pathetically scurried after the scraps of love I now get thrown like pieces of unwanted food.

But I must have been near the end of being enough for her. The earliest in that range would have been boys who went to the same college, friends and acquaintances she fell into bed with, because how they could they not? Logistics enable many sloppy loves. Next would have been the boys, maybe considered men, those in their post-collegiate days, not so serious but finding their way, just getting careers in business, with a decent apartment and no longer living with "other dudes" or smoking so much weed, playing video games, but only on weekends. One of these, Julia could've seen. The last of her possibilities would have been someone like me, those over 30 with slightly nicer cars, maybe with some money in the bank, with more life experience. I might have been recognized as him, though I held on with my fingernails at the edge of a cliff to call myself by that name.

For Julia to respond to my first message could have just been my pictures. I would later change them to show clearly, in color, how much hair I did or did not have and how much fat around the middle I accumulated. But the old ones, the black and whites ones—though I never asked any of those I met— must have been more impressive. I must have appeared more youthful than I was.

Julia's profile was immensely charming and mentioned her love of opera. One of her pictures was a selfie at a ballgame on a clear night, beer in one hand, a headband pulling back her golden hair. She noted her love of cheese in her profile, so I messaged her about my love of it when fried.

"We should enjoy some together sometime and eat cheese."

"That could be arranged," she messaged back, and so it was.

At a wine bar in the summer at night I watched cars drive by as I waited for Christine. Sitting on a bike rack near tall potted plants, lamps lit the sidewalk where couples sat in pairs. The night was warm. I overheard someone discuss the latest *This American Life*. Nearer our meeting time I went inside and ordered a beer, trying to appear like I belonged.

Julia did not send a text to say she would be late, though she would be by about fifteen minutes. She walked in wearing a leather jacket and a turquoise skirt with black tights. Red lipstick too, and I knew, if things went well, I would be lucky. Would we marry? That is the question I always ask in the first moment I see the other. We would not, but I would want to see Julia without her black leather jacket and short turquoise skirt and black tights, that I also knew. A brief hug, and we got a table. Julia ordered a glass of white wine as I drank my beer.

"So you closed out your tab?" she asked as she put away her card wallet in her purse.

"Am I supposed to?" I said, then took a drink.

"Right," she said. I kept looking at her. "Wait," she said, "you're kidding, right?"

"Am I supposed to be?" I took another drink.

"You pay for what you get at the bar, *at the bar*, the tip goes with the bartender." She wanted to roll her eyes, I could tell. We were off to a bad start.

"Sorry, didn't know that." I got up, pushing my chair back and squishing my face into my neck at the same time.

"Really?" she said, rhetorically.

"Well," I said walking away, "I'm a naive farm boy." It was, at the time, my profile name.

As I went to take care of the bill, I imagine now but could not then because I was too embarrassed to think of anything other than how I had screwed up, Julia texting her friends with something like, "Disaster."

It must have been the wine. By the end of the night after I heard stories of life at the Peabody Institute in Maryland where Julia "basically, just sang," and where she lived in Uptown across from *Pizza Luce*, and the two girls who worked as waitresses and she lived with, I overcame what I had lost at the beginning. Julia was smiling. Her lips were deeply red.

"You don't have to do that," she said as she dug in her purse, even after the waitress had picked up the check, along with my card.

"Too late," I said.

"Sneaky," she said, and I did not deny that, even if it wasn't true.

By her bike, her chain lock tied around a No Parking sign down the street.

"You're sure you're okay to ride this home?" I patted the seat. "I can give you a ride."

"I'm gooood." And she put on her helmet. It puffed out her cheeks, making her seem even younger than she was. We hugged goodbye, which turned into kissing. Julia wore so much, I tasted her lipstick. Then she rode away. It must have been like riding sober in the daytime, like a schoolgirl going home from school.

A couple days later, since Julia and I talked at length about musicals, we decided to watch the one with Bjork. Julia in the suburbs, sitting beside me on my landlord's couch, and no matter how serious the movie became, I could not keep myself away from her gorgeous, meaty legs, wrapped up in white woolen tights. And her neck, under her hair, I was kissing her in the space below her ear. All the while, horrifically sad things unfolded on the television in front of us.

"I need to watch this," Julia would say and pat me off, and I would relent, until we kissed again more intently. After the movie I took her back to Uptown, where we stayed in my car in front of her brick apartment building.

"You should come over this weekend," she said, my windows fogged over. She wanted to watch *Don Giovanni* to show me the role she played in college, and so she could challenge me on how much whiskey I could drink. I agreed. She did not need to twist my arm.

The night we watched the opera, Julia wore a yellow dress—snug around her waist—and red lipstick and her perfume. It wafted through the living room by the abstract art on the walls and the mirror for her and the other young women to check themselves out before going out every night. A stuffed gorilla sat next to an electric piano. Julia and I had our glasses filled to the brim. The lights on, we stood by the gorilla as I reached down and played one of the few chords I know. I asked if I could hear her sing.

"I don't know," she said. "The people downstairs get really pissed. And it's fucked up because these are the same people who have these loud parties until like six in the morning. But if I play my piano and sing in the afternoon they have a shitfit."

I took a big drink. "I'm beating you." I showed Julia my glass.

"Whatever," she said and took an even bigger one.

"So are we going to watch this or what?"

"Dude," she said. "Guys say they wanna watch this, but then when they watch it and they are like super bored."

"I'm a big boy, Julia. I wouldn't say I wanted to watch it if I didn't." And that was maybe, at best, half true.

"Alllriiiight." She slapped my butt and went and flopped down in front of the TV. I sat on the couch and watched her hit the buttons, swearing. "Our set-up is so ghetto," she said.

"You sure you know how to work that thing?" I asked.

"Shut it, boy," she said, flipping me off without turning around, still pushing buttons with her other hand. I looked forward to her coming back to the couch. I was unsure if I belonged in her Uptown apartment, but I was so glad to be there.

Julia figured it out and got up and turned off the lights. We sank into each other. In darkness we watched, and though I didn't say as much—as I hoped I would be different from the other boys—the opera did bore me. It seemed to me a dry reinvention, like it belonged in a stuffy museum. Mostly we drank and kissed. Her skirt above her waist, I felt the smoothness created from her crotch and underwear. She pulled away. I thought that was it.

"Wanna just go to my room?" she asked.

"Yes," I said. "Yeah." Just steps away, it was a make-shift space meant as an office. With French glass doors, it hardly fit a double bed, a dresser and a bookshelf. I sat on her creaky bed as she went to refill our drinks. When she returned, she set them down, and I marveled as she slipped off into nothing. She had a powerful body with tight breasts, and I would like to say I gave her the night of her life. I would like to say I made Julia come a thousand times. If I am honest, I know I did not, but for a few moments, we were restful. I thought it would be enough for a first time. I thought Julia would be like Hannah, or even Lindsey.

"But you can go again, right?" Julia asked, shattering the silence. "I mean, that's not it."

"Just need rest a little," I said and maneuvered to my side of her bed, nearly falling off. I pretended to be asleep. I don't know when, but I woke to Julia kicking her legs and thrashing her arms.

"Fuck you," she said, "fuck you for coming. I can't believe this shit. Fuck you." Through the window, and not so far in the distance, I heard yelling, like a mating call. Eventually, Julia muttered. She tired and fell asleep.

In the morning we tried again, and it was better, as if the alcohol put a demon in us. In the gentle hush afterward, Julia admitted she had never come, so as I drove away down her crowded street, I felt relieved. Others had tried and failed too. Later that week, Julia invited me to the city. We went to the Stone Arch Bridge.

Walking across holding hands, from downtown to northeast Minneapolis across the Mississippi River, we saw in the tranquil night the last vestiges of old mills, crumbling like Roman cities. We went through the small park on a romantic cobblestone road past an old Pillsbury factory bulging out of its foundation, the façade supported by massive braces. Further, we strolled along start-up business and condos with incredibly expensive brick walls. And we talked, for the most part about how Julia believed I didn't get out enough. It may sound regressive of me, but I thought of Hannah.

In the time after that, we did city things. Julia and I went to bars with no parking, restaurants with one word in their title, movie theaters playing movies no one ever saw outside of New York or Los Angeles, maybe Seattle or Chicago. I was anxious through it all. Our sex never became great. So we ended, with a whimper, not a bang. Julia stopped answering my calls and I stopped calling. I never asked why. Which is a privilege, I think, to understand intuitively the reasons why you can't be with someone. The other way it can end, shrouded in vague allusions, is much worse.

A month or so after it was over, I did hear from Julia. At that time, I was in the midst of the getting to know the last person I would ever need to know, I thought, and because of that I did not think much of what Julia said. Though if she had sent what she sent weeks later, I would've paid more attention. It came around two in the morning.

"Yes!" is all it said, not in response to anything I asked. I had not texted her for almost five weeks. The question was her and I, and the answer was the one in her bed that night. I imagine him hard as a rock, as big as a mule.

CHAPTER FIFTEEN

My soul had begun to fade. I did not know guilt when I was still seeing Julia and received a reply from Yalzelia. Caitlin was her real name, a woman who, I assumed, had missed out on her chance. I have never conducted an experiment to prove it, but the most alive and bright and willing to take a chance on love are not in their late 20s. In those odd years, an unknown cut makes us too jaded. It is the ones on either side of these ages who go to love with a fresher heart.

My useless theory had no bearing on Yalzelia, her sarcastic profile peppered with oblique references to left field rap music. She attended Yale, though as we sent emails back and forth that week, she vacationed in Wyoming. Everything about her was very cool. It's the word I would use, even if I knew every other word in the world, cool. I liked Caitlin from the start, even if she waved warning flags from that same beginning.

"We'll see," she replied to my asking her out. "I'm back late Tuesday night, but I have another date Wednesday with a guy who got directly to the point."

But "directly to the point" must have been forgotten, because I picked Caitlin up on that Wednesday. I took the full moon as a good sign as I waited by my car. Before that moment, I had known ups and downs, but nothing could make me flag in my pursuit. I had the experience of Hannah. She had proved it was possible for someone to want me for a lifetime. I know, if I had been more amenable to the word, she would have said she loved me.

When Caitlin emerged from a dark path by the side of the house, I assumed good things. But it was bad, right from the start. Her first motion was a nod, then a hello, and by the way Caitlin greeted me, forcing a tight smile, I knew we would have a difficult time. I am sure this type of immediate feeling is known by others. I cannot be the only one.

"Glad you made it," I said, pushing myself for something else to say, "sorry about your car. That really stinks." She had hit a deer, totaled it on the way back to Minneapolis from her trip to Wyoming.

"Thanks," she said, and that was all she said. We got in the car. I drove her to the suburbs.

We should have never met, Caitlin and I. Before the internet, we would have never done so. Our paths would have never crossed. Caitlin, too experienced, needed an art director at an advertising agency who is in charge of people who create in pods. And I needed, well, I needed someone who was not Caitlin, someone who laughed at my stupidities and is gracious in regards to my social standing until I reached my own version of making it.

I wanted to shout to her that I was sorry, breaking the silence of the car, "The internet has tricked smarter people than us!" Caitlin, I know, would not have fought it. She would've thanked me. My pride fought back, so I said nothing.

In the suburbs, my landlord—a rarely gregarious type—was cleaning up in the kitchen, and that night for some reason he was also drinking and dancing around and singing. I think he saved us. Nothing had been planned other than watch television. Which made me think, before arriving, that I was really great. Caitlin wants be alone with me. I never considered the opposite, that she wanted to keep me hidden.

With the landlord, we had some laughs. Caitlin, nearing 30, had collagen-infused lips, a pulled-back face, and wore black tights with layers of black clothes, the same as her dyed black hair. She told us about her private school and how she was thousands of dollars in debt, even if she worked as a technical writer for a large, successful firm.

We moved to the living room and watched internet videos. Caitlin and I sat closer when my landlord went to bed and soon her legs became entwined in mine. I squeezed her soft thigh, making me long for Julia or Lindsey's more substantial ones, then she was on top of me. We did everything we could with our clothes on. I thought, yes, a Yale girl with dyed hair and collagen lips and a writing job, even if she hated me, will be mine.

"Should we go upstairs?" she asked, breathing out. "It won't take long." As if we were taking out the garbage.

"I don't have any condoms," I said. But I did, I just could not risk things going poorly. I wanted Caitlin again. I needed time, I could tell, to show her how great I could be. When she heard my answer, she got off and straightened her hair. She asked if I could drive her home.

On the way, somehow, Caitlin compared the sensation of liquid going through a straw to semen going through the shaft of a penis. How we got on that subject, I have no idea. But we did.

"You know," she said, "you can just tell it's coming." Begrudgingly, it made a lot of sense.

We dryly kissed goodbye at Caitlin's back door, just sort of pecking. We hugged too, the kind cousins give each other, then she went inside, and that was the last time I saw her. Though if I am being honest, I did not think that would be it. We had nearly done the most intimate thing two people can do. We had gotten past our rough patch. We went through something. That could not be the end. It was, but it was also a beginning.

CHAPTER SIXTEEN

I cannot imagine a hotter bed. Even in Hannah's crumbling art house with no insulation where the windows never fully shut and there were cracks in the ceiling, it had no equal. We heard birds between the drywall and the siding once. Hannah lived in the attic, but she loved it. I drove there after work.

Going down Franklin, turning right at her street with a garage on the corner that had a mural of Jesus looking as if he received fellatio from one of his followers, down that street full of potholes from the winter before. At midnight I got out and walked to her front door, the heat enveloping me. It would be hotter in her bedroom, so when I got up there I was not surprised to see Hannah's wet hair dangling over the side of the bed. Like a cat, she stretched out as long as possible. Remember, we had gotten back together.

"Holy Hannah, Hannah," I said and she always at least gave me a smile. Her face all red, she stood up and put her arms around me.

"Robbies, oh my goodness, can I come over to your place tomorrow? It was so hot today I went to a movie just so I could just sit in air conditioning."

"Yes yes, my Hannah." We were good like that for a short time. I took off my shoes and shirt. "So how was your trip out east? Looks like it was real lavish."

She had gone to the mansion house of her uncle and sent a picture to me every day with her new phone.

"Oh Robbies, it was so nice. His house is amazing. It has its own beach and he bought a yacht. We sailed during the day and ate out every night, except for the one night he cooked lobster." Then she said in a lilting way, like a song, "You should've come."

"I know," I said. "I should have."

Hannah undressed too, and her skin had become brown from vacation, everywhere except for where she wore a two-piece suit, so her bottom and breasts were all white. I tried to deny how good that looked as we put only a thin white sheet over us on the bed. Hannah turned on a movie. We watched on her laptop as I tried to keep my distance. If I got too close, Hannah would touch me in the places she knew to touch and I would be incapable of resisting. The more we did those things, the harder it would be to break up. It was coming again soon. She began to crawl her hands down my stomach and to my waist, to my inner thighs, then she stopped.

"What is this?" She pushed the laptop off of us.

"What's what?"

"This," she said. "Right here. Feel."

"Feel what?"

So she guided me, and the feeling made me jump out of bed. I went over to Hannah's full-body mirror and there it was, as I raised my sac, a lump the size of a raisin. Just as soon I let go of my scrotum, I turned off the light and came back to bed. In the darkness, looking up at her ceiling, Hannah was in my arms as I tried to say in earnest, "Not a big deal. that kind of thing can't just pop up like that, I don't think."

Hannah squeezed me tighter as she said, "Robbies, no, you have to get that checked out."

I wanted to put my face on my pillow to avoid the conversation. I badly wanted to. I stayed motionless as I said, "Okay, but I'm sure it's not a big deal."

Hannah kissed me, glad I had said yes, but I did know what I had agreed to do. I would be going to the doctor to see if I had cancer? Hannah fell asleep first, and as I listened to her breathe, I imagined what being dead would be like.

The next night in the suburbs, and it was cooler there. My landlord had air conditioning, even if he never did like to turn it down too low. I had called for an appointment and would be going in the morning. With Hannah in bed, I talked with my doctor friend, Ben. He was in Chicago and I was in a bathroom in the suburbs of Minneapolis as I asked him how, exactly, something like this could happen.

"It was all of a sudden there. Is that even possible? And it doesn't hurt. Isn't it supposed to hurt?"

"You said it was on the outside?" Ben asked.

"I think, but does it start from the inside?" I had no idea. In the bathroom, I pulled it up so I could see.

"I don't know for sure if I can't see what's going on, but I think you're okay. I'd still go and check, though."

I picked at it. "Alright, man, thanks," my voice straining from pinching. "Thanks."

My friend hung up first. With the phone between my shoulders and my ear, I took a flap of skin and squeezed hard. A small stream of puss oozed out.

At work that night I had floated on an uneasy pocket of air, touching it when no one was looking, knowing my life was over but I had not done a single thing with it. Those worries began to evaporate as I went upstairs to tell Hannah about what happened in the bathroom.

"But we're still going to go in the morning, right? We want you to make sure, okay?"

"We do," I said and gave Hannah a kiss. I wanted her. As much as I had before and never would again.

The next morning we went to the doctor's office, and with all the construction, I was thankful to have Hannah as my navigator. What a comfort for her to be there and help me with the questionnaire form in the lobby, to give me a kiss when they called my name. She smiled with encouragement when my name got called.

I looked back and there was a magazine in her lap, but she was looking at me.

The doctor's visit might go on record as the shortest testicle examination ever, notable only for the most shrunken penis in the history of time. The elderly doctor did manage, somehow, to take hold of my balls and did see that it was, indeed, a pimple. All the heat that summer, that was it.

Yet still I left relieved, not embarrassed. I had Hannah, and we existed in unspoken harmony. But while we rode the elevator down in the quiet, it struck me. What if she wasn't with me? What if after she leaves, something significant happens and I don't know what to do? What if I am always too afraid to be alone? What if the world ends, as it seemed it would that summer and even into fall with as hot as it was, and I am left to scavenge and wander and fend for myself? Will I die in the first week? First day?

A light rain fell as I drove, and I began to forget. Hannah pointed out clubs we had not yet been to, the places we should have already gone. By the time we arrived at the Malaysian restaurant, it rained hard, pelting against the windows. I wanted to express to Hannah how much what she had done had meant, but I couldn't. I don't think she knew, or knows now. And that's good, I think, I did not want her to feel like another who got it wrong, instead of the only one who got it right, to be by my side.

"Really, though, thank you. I feel a lot better." I took a bite of food and acted as if I had just eaten my favorite thing in the whole world.

"I'm just glad I could be here, Robbies." She ate too, and I think we were very happy.

Back at her place that day, we were together on her swirling desk chair. Hannah lifted up her dress and it was lovely and raw in a really good way. With that memory, going to work, I was a man. I drove knowing I had a family who would not be in debt for the rest of their lives because of me. My nieces and nephews would have prosperous lives.

For the whole of my shift at the drug factory, I thought about Hannah. About how my landlord and her would be in the suburbs on the weekends, and as the night dipped into morning we would be watching internet videos, singing 90s R&B songs. I thought of the day I got back from Chicago where I visited my friend, waiting at the airport pick up lane alone, and there was Hannah coming to pick me up. The rest of that day was idyllic at the beach. Leaves in the high branches and the blue sky dotted with listless clouds as we laid on the comfortable grass. I thought as well of when we would cook on the weekends, and whenever my landlord went to his parents' house, Hannah would wear only an apron.

Hannah often said our bodies fit together perfectly. She liked my chest hair, even my balding head. She commented, more than once, that she just could not understand why I never grew it out. I remember I did not kiss her each time she said that. That seems like a crime now.

CHAPTER SEVENTEEN

Megan Jones, Anne Smith, Jenny Erickson, these are the names I have always known. They are the ones I should have stuck to. A name like Amariah Schwartzman, I think if I had to speak for a younger mind, I believed it would be different. With time as my aid, I could say that's true. Also, with time or eternity or all the gods both old and new, I could say that is not true at all.

I remember seeing her profile. It was after Caitlin, when I began to have the creeping sense going online to find someone would never work. It was too easy, the way the website expedited love. It was wrong to always have a new supply of flesh replacing the old supply.

We had found way to search for a partner to spend a lifetime with without leaving our homes. We had been given too much power. Each one of us with a password to a program where we could click a button, and hours later—or even minutes—be lying underneath another worrying if maybe we should not have done the thing we just did, and to think, 80 years in the future, we might have something walking, talking, thinking, dreading their own death, because one night 80 years before we were bored and on the internet.

That week when I saw Amariah's profile was the first time that idea crept into my head, though I hope I am not thought of as ignorant. I had, after all, mostly positive experiences until then. Yes I had let someone down, but I had been let down too, and I chalked that up to naivety. Everything must come to its level, is what I thought.

Amariah, RiahS as she named herself online, stalked my profile several times that week in early December, which jolted me. It made me rethink myself. Here was the archetype: dense curly hair, a unique nose, and dark features, and the added bonuses of dimples and a lithe figure. On God's green earth, there was no reason for RiahS to be with me. Just too attractive, is what I thought.

I had other irons: a recent college graduate who wore a Paul Bunyan outfit in her profile picture, replete with short shorts and a toy ax and flannel shirt. She worked as a director at a Jewish summer camp, and I think I might have loved her without knowing her. And Bernice, someone who, based upon her profile, could have been my wife, with freckles, chocolate hair and a goofy smile. We had been messaging for almost a month, and I kept going because she seemed so interesting. I had all these and more, making the thought of RiahS secondary, even unreasonable. I like to think, if nothing else, I am that much. I am reasonable.

But as maybe Hashem Himself would have it, Amariah looked at my profile one last time, tipping my ledgers, so that on a Saturday afternoon after return-ing from a second-hand clothing store, I decided to do it. It was why she was there, after all, to receive random messages from strangers. So I went to her profile, and in her six things she could "never do without," after dogs and running and crushed red pepper and traveling and bars with patios or rooftops, she mentioned something unique.

"Deals."

Often, in that space, there is faux indignation, or the question is just left blank. If not that, the most obvious is stated—air, water, family, friends. But in the rarest cases there is the route of Amariah's, the most interesting, listing what is precious or noteworthy beyond what others might think precious or noteworthy.

And yes Amariah was Jewish, but I didn't know that. I hadn't dated Hannah because she was Jewish. It just happened to be that the things which made her Jewish—post-religious, good-looking, educated—overlapped. Amariah had the same traits, in a younger and fitter form, back from a year in Thailand. Her time overseas, however, I could not have cared less about that, everyone on that site has gone overseas. I wanted to talk deals, so I wrote my message. It's funny; we had such an innocent beginning.

Amariah wrote back the next day, a Sunday, and my heart sung, seeing the red heart in my inbox. I forgot everything. My average job. My failures with others. My life as a man in his thirties without a wife or children and living in the suburbs. Everything vanished with the bright newness of Amariah.

"Those are some good deals," she wrote. "You seem like the kind of guy who writes. Are you a writer? Let's talk soon."

I made allusions in my profile to what I did, but I never came out and explicitly said anything about factory work. So I gave her a coded answer, though I wanted to tell Amariah my life story right then and there. I wanted to hear her say every decision I ever made was right. They led me to her.

That Sunday afternoon, sitting in a plush reclining chair, my landlord on his computer, the Vikings game on, and looking out at the trace snow on the lawn—a milder winter than the last—I could not believe it. I had found the love of my life.

Ben, my friend in Chicago studying to be a doctor, came to town that week. He was to interview for a position as a resident at a hospital in Minneapolis, and before I went to pick him up at the airport, I forgot to text Amariah. We had yet to meet, but it seemed as if I didn't respond to her texts on time, she would get upset. It was crazy to think, I understand, but when I got back from the airport she had sent me not one, but two messages.

"You're being very undude," the second said, referencing a movie we both liked. Soon we would take our profiles down. That was easy to see.

Days later at a bar near her house on a frigid evening. I parked a couple blocks away, and as I walked I felt I had taken a dreamy, hallucinogenic drug, thinking of the hours to come. Inside to the right was a jukebox and a circular table to the left. A long row of booths and an equally lonely row of bar stools on the other. This was a townie bar, even if it lived near bars where men from local up-and-coming bands worked as bartenders. I sat in one of the booths, wearing my suit jacket and a blue dress shirt to look my best, then it happened, she walked in. She twirled around once, looking for her date, and spotted me. We hugged and I could not believe how she smelled, as my wife would. We sat down.

"Suit jacket, what's up with that?" she asked as she took off her coat. "We're going downtown after this?" Her smile was perfect, yes that too.

"Oh, this?" I said. "Just something I threw on."

We ordered drinks and began to talk about those we had seen from the website. We were doing so to reminisce about our single pasts. Soon that is all they would be.

"You're nothing like him," Amariah was saying. "You look your age." Amariah had explained to me her worst online date. "That guy was at least five or six years older, if not more." She took another drink of her vodka tonic through a straw.

"So who else?" I wanted to know every possibility, like a head coach needs to know everything about the competition before a big game, so as to crush it.

"Are you sure? Amariah asked, giving me an out. "I mean, is this weird?"

"No-no," I said, "people do this." And that made her smile, her dimples forming on either side of her mouth.

"Fun," she said, as if talking with one of her girl-friends. "Well, let's see, there were some guys last week, but nothing serious. Then I went on a couple dates with a law student. Those were the most boring dates I've ever been on, Robert. Seriously, I hope you haven't dated any lawyers. I'm sorry, have you?"

"Maybe one or two," I said, trying to keep up.

"One or two, I hope they weren't *so* bad." She looked at me in a way, I think, that said she would kiss me, or I would kiss her, that we would kiss. Centering herself across from me, like in a school photo, she swirled her drink with her straw. "And then there's this guy in med school. I should tell him it isn't going to work. How many dates do you have to go on before you can't text break up anymore?"

"Two, I guess... three?" The others dropped like flies. "Anyone else I should worry about?" I could say that. I could get away with it. It was our connection.

"A couple more," she said. "One is a fisherman, actually."

"A fisherman? Sounds like a real jerk."

Amariah slapped my hand. "Oh he's not so bad. He teaches wrestling too. And I'm kinda into that whole brawny thing."

"I could take 'em." And I flexed my right bicep, pushed it toward her over the table to feel.

"Hmm," she said as she did. "That's nice, but he is pretty big." I had not known Amariah for more than an hour and I wanted to bare-knuckle box this fisherman. I wanted our fight to be to the death.

Soon, we had finished our drinks. Two beers for me and three mixed drinks for her. We held hands over the table as she breathed in my scarf.

"So good," she said, then after that she got up to go to the bathroom and told me to look at her ass as she walked away. Maybe it was the alcohol, but it was most hearty thing I had ever seen.

We walked out after I paid the bill. And how good she looked, tall and cosmopolitan, exiting with me as if we were Manhattanites in the early 60s on Madison Avenue. On the sidewalk she drew closer, shielding her thin body against the wind. I wore a farmer's coat, cloth with warm liner, and she had her hand down one of its pockets. When we got to my car, I turned on the seat warmers and said, "I've wanted to do this all night."

"What's that," Amariah said. "Kiss…" Then we did. She kissed my neck as I drove her home. In front of her brother's house, we grabbed at each other.

"Here," she said as she turned her eye-watering back-side toward me. "Get a better feel." So I did, and whatever sins I committed in life, they were forgiven.

"Wait a second," she said after more. "I've never kissed a boy in a back seat. But I kinda want to. You want to?"

"Yeah," I said. "We could do that." So we piled out, and before I could think of what to do next, Amariah faced me, her hair obscuring the back window. After we both finished, I walked her inside.

"You can't come in." We kissed by the side of her brother's house in the cold. I held her arms above her head. "I want you to, but you can't."

But we did not stop. Later, at last letting go of each other, we walked our separate ways not looking ahead, but behind. Back home, both of us under separate blankets, we talked on the phone for an hour. We texted until we fell asleep. It was how life was supposed to be.

CHAPTER EIGHTEEN

"Does Petite Chanteuse make bomb oatmeal cook-ies?"

This was the text from Amariah in the morning. Petite Chanteuse was Bernice, with whom I had a date that night, and I would have canceled it if Amariah had wanted me to.

"Maybe," I typed back from bed. "You'll just have to bring some to karaoke and I can judge."

We planned to go out with Amariah's friends after my date. The next day after that, as Amariah told me at the bar, she had a date with fisherman. But it was not supposed to matter. Neither of us was supposed to care.

"We're taking our dogs to the dog parks," Amariah told me. This was after she smelled my scarf. "He has the most adorable dog in the world. You should see it, Rob." Though I could not imagine a scenario in this life where I would ever want to see this man's dog.

By the afternoon the next day we had planned for Amariah to bring her friends to karaoke and I would bring my landlord, with the caveat being, as Amariah detailed, "You can NOT stay at my brother's place. And I'm not staying in the 'burbs. So you'll just have to dream of me when you go home." Then a winking emoticon.

Bernice and I did go our date that night, though neither of us was as sparkly as our profiles. She told a long story about a mix up of desserts at her old job, and I told her about the factory and nothing else. Though when I left that night, where I would have normally felt a pit of despair, I knew thankfulness. My aim was true, and from Bernice I went to pick up Amariah. I can see her still as she walks down the still, cold sidewalk of her brother's house. She wears a red stocking hat with a tassel, a black coat and white gloves, and when she gets in my car, we have a kiss.

As the dome light faded away, she pulled out a plastic baggie.

"Here, try one." She put one of the cookies in my mouth like I was a parrot. "What do you think?"

"Good," I mumbled as she took my hand. We did let go until I had to park.

Inside the karaoke bar, I bought the drinks while Amariah secured us a table. In the back with the pool table, the regulars up front, my drink in one hand while the other ran along her thigh over black tights.

"It was fine," I said about Bernice. "But she was…she was just a bit heavier. And she didn't really have much to say other than her stories about waitressing, even if she's a freelance writer now? I will say this, though, Amariah, Bernice did wear a high-waisted skirt."

"A pencil skirt? On the first date? *Petite Chanteuse*," Amariah said in a mock French accent, then back to English, "She's a French ho, fo sho."

I was laughing as I said, "But it looked good. And I haven't seen you wear one. I'm beginning to think you don't have any."

"Buddy, I'll wear one. But not just any night." She leaned in and we kissed as I squeezed her thigh. I felt its muscle, its fat, the beginning of her warmth. We even did that pathetic nose cuddling couples do. At that moment, I almost found the courage to tell her not to go on her date with the fisherman. I was very close.

When my landlord came, we got a table near the front. Amariah and I whispered in each other ears, holding hands except for she when went up to sing a duet with her bestie—who flopped around the stage—and when I sang an R&B song from the 90s After we drank and sang, we decided to leave, forgetting what was planned. Amariah was finishing her last song of the night—"Killing Me Softly"—and as the clapping died, I whisked her away. She waved to everyone in the bar like a beauty queen in a parade. It was a joke, I know, but I thought it was beautiful.

Halfway home in the cab, Amariah was facing out the back window and kissing my neck. When we got to house in the suburbs, we collapsed on the couch. I fed her saltines and water. We feel asleep on each other. In the middle of the night I woke and lifted her to bed. She had the mass of a person, awkward and hard to manage but light, with slim hips and tiny breasts, except for the weight she kept in her bottom. At the top of my stairs, she woke.

"Okay, okay," she said, "you can put me down. We get it."

With the lights off, we did what we did. After, I thought of the cloudy afternoons and bright mornings, the dusky evenings when I would see her in the light. To study her body until there was not a part of it I did not know better than my own. In the morning, Amariah called her bestie. Next to her in bed, I could hear the other phone ringing.

"If I don't call her," Amariah said, "she calls me. It's cute, isn't it?" Picking up one of her fingers, I let it drop on my chest like the beat of a drum.

"Oh I should, should I?" I heard later. Amariah whispered in my ear, "She told me to give you a bj." Amariah then said to her friend, "I don't give bjs out on the second date." Then she looked at me. "I'm a lady."

We went back to each other after the call, and it was all I could want. Spent, we watched videos from the internet. After that we dressed and my landlord took us back to my car. From the karaoke bar, I took her home. Not yet noon, we sat there in my warming vehicle beside her brother's house.

"You know," I said, hoping she would understand what I was trying to say. "We could go get breakfast, go see a movie or something? I don't have anywhere to be today." It was Saturday. She held the door, her head inside. Warm and cold air mixed between us.

"I know, but I need to, Robert. I'll see you again, okay?" She pulled in and kissed me, and I watched her walk back up her brother's sidewalk. I hope, if someone had told the one watching that was the last time he would see her, he would've done something. I hope he would've had courage.

That evening, Amariah went out to Uptown and so did I. I thought we could met, and when my phone started buzzing, I was sure we would. Stepping away from my group, I had the confidence of someone who believed he possessed a girlfriend who is more fit and attractive and smarter than most other girlfriends in the world.

"Hey!" her text said. "I don't think tonight is a good night. The fisherman and I are still kinda hanging out and I want to see what he's like when he's drunk and dancing. Call me!"

I had been punched, and I wandered out of the bar, back to where I last remembered my car being. I think I drove home, though it is hard to say for sure. I may have floated or flown or swam. I may have parked my car by my bed. That's where I was with my phone.

Take your time, Robert, just a word or two, express disinterest. No, don't come off as sarcastic, she'll be able to detect, deeper down, that desire, and that will make her shy away because what woman would want to be with a man who would get so hurt over such a thing? In the end I decided on sending her nothing, and by the next morning, a Sunday, I opened my phone to see a message sent at two in the morning.

"Burn," is all it said.

"Burn?" I replied right away. "You were out with another guy, right? I like you, Amariah, so when you tell me you're out with someone else, it's kind of weird."

She did not reply. It was overcast that day, and I tried to watch football to get my mind off of things. But it was no use. It got so bad I ran the idea by my landlord of going to see Amariah at her part-time job at a coffee shop in Uptown.

"What would you say," he said. The usual things surrounded him: cat, computer, foods like meats and breads. "Hi Amariah, guy you've seen twice is here, come and talk to me now."

My landlord convinced me. I did nothing but wait, because one in love is the one who waits, even if I always found that word too serious. When Amariah responded later that afternoon, I was so relieved, I slumped down in my chair.

"Fair enough," she wrote. "And I did just get off work. I've got coffee grounds in my boots." And she ended her message with a smiley face.

"Nice," I wrote back with too much alacrity. "How was last night?"

"Pretty good. It was fun, sweaty."

I was in the kitchen when I read that, and it compelled me to mix a large drink, too strong for a Sunday night. Later, I went to her profile. She was online at that moment, so I sent a text, and this is what it said, "You're awfully cavalier with love, aren't you, Amariah?"

Seconds later was her reply, as if Amariah kept a copy of it for situations like ours. At the end she wrote "…and this is just too much, too soon."

The room spun as I immediately called her. I called again, and again received the prerecorded voice. Collapsing in bed, I punched at my keyboard, tracing the indention of my soul, and after I wrote my email I passed out. In the morning, my heart pounding and my head a cloudy mess, I had a reply. Her profile was the same as weeks before, but this time it seemed more like a harbinger of something dark, not bright.

"…And he has dogs," Amariah wrote. "Which I really like. He even has a flippin' family farm outside Northfield. You're right to bring up the age thing too. Even though I know I said I don't care what other people think of who I'm with, that is important. I want someone I can bring home and introduce to my friends and family and the fisherman is just a lot closer in age. We're trying to figure things out after college, so I think it makes more sense to do it together than to try and start with someone older who's already on his path. That doesn't mean I don't ever want to see you again, but right now I think we should just take a little break. You're a great guy. Love, Amariah."

In reply I sent two emails, one that morning, then another in the afternoon after Amariah looked at my profile again. I emailed her the week for the same reason, then texted her when she looked at my profile once more. I asked if she wanted to get coffee and talk. But my messages floated, out in an abyss with so many failed others. Days after that, Amariah looked at my profile. It happened to be Sunday afternoon and I had just heard speaker online talking about taking what you want instead of wishing for it, so I sent another text, one I constructed for a solid hour about going out with some friends of mine in town from Seattle. They knew a bartender who worked near Amariah's brother's place.

"And he's in Tapes N Tapes (Oooh la la). So it'll be fun and chill. Please don't close your heart, Amariah."

Not waiting for a reply, I left to the grocery store and got flowers, the same ones I bought Hannah on the day of her puppet theater. After I parked on the street near the bar, I opened my phone. It had lit up on the way, but I couldn't bring myself to look.

"This isn't happening," she wrote. "I got really turned off by how intense things got."

I threw the flowers on a nearby lawn and drove back to the suburbs.

Christmas came soon after and going home heartened me. To awaken from my self-loathing by seeing family. To eat good food, to drown in unconditional love. But as my sister and her husband and I watched a movie, my phone clutched in my hand, it lit up once again.

"Merry Christmas Rob." At first I thought it was a joke, but in the morning I replied to Amariah by asking how everything was. She replied.

"Great!" she wrote. An exclamation, she had sent an exclamation. I sensed everything slipping back toward me. So I texted her again, but received nothing. I texted once more a day later, and nothing, not until New Year's

Eve with a few friends back in Minneapolis did I get her next message.

"Your profile changes are ridiculous," she texted. "Happy New Year's."

Rejuvenated once again, I slipped away from the New Year's party. Standing by the stove, expectant, I called her, but her phone just rang. I thought up the most reasonable possibilities for why. Maybe she couldn't pick up because she had to consider the things she wanted to say. Or maybe her phone wasn't even by her. Maybe she had set it down for the night and would call in the morning. Eventually, my excuses for us ran out. Another drunken night by my computer, after seeing she had changed her profile picture to one from a New Year's party, I decided to do it. Now I should preface this and say I am not a poet, but there was a time when I wanted to be one. So I emailed her my poem, adding in my message, "and don't text me anymore, please, if I'm just a guy you keep at the end of a string to see how long I can hang. I want no part it."

By morning there were two messages from Amariah's deleted account. In the first, she agreed to my request. Minutes after, she wrote, "Actually, thinking about it, it's not cool to write that blog post or whatever that shit was supposed to be. Fuck off."

So that's what I did.

CHAPTER NINETEEN

As a way of mending, I sought the affection of others. I wanted to sink in touches. Smother me in breasts and butts and stomachs and necks and smells and noises. Send me down in a bucket to the well of good feelings. If I drown there, that's fine, at least I'll be happy in my last moments, rather than exhausted and dehydrated after running for years toward a mirage.

I sent a text to Bernice first. Somehow I still had her as a contact. As a mode of self-preservation, I delete all these numbers. Never do I want to find myself on some Friday evening scrolling through a list of names that are not going to answer. For some reason, Bernice sat there waiting. Perhaps she had been crying for me. Maybe she never called because she was just too broken up.

"That sounds quite lovely," Bernice texted in regards to the movie I suggested. "Unfortunately, currently, my schedule vehemently disagrees."

Vehemently is what killed me. I deleted her number.

But there were more. CaliMNGurl, though her real name was Jan, I think. Her pictures I remember more clearly, one where is standing in a field of sunflowers as the sun sets, smiling the toothiest smile, as a wife would smile on her wedding day. In another she is with her brother—according to the caption—wearing overalls, both with their thumbs in their pockets. She wears a straw hat and sticks out one cowboy boot, like in a hoe-down, and again, she is smiling so much. Then she is in a kitchen with a freshly-baked pie and her smile is almost too generous, indulgent even. My heart was too exposed after Amariah when I messaged CaliMNGurl, its dust flaking over my words. But Jan, I think that was her name, brushed them away. She responded to my message about the politics of online dating.

"I just don't view the first date as a first date, that's a pre-date to see if you even want to go on a real date. I always suggest a ten-minute coffee or something like that, that way we know if it's going anywhere. If it's not, we can both be on our way and not have wasted time. I don't want this to be a game. That's when people's feelings get hurt."

How great it was! To breathe in fresh air from CaliMNGurl, possibly her name was Jan, a redhead with freckles. I asked for soup instead of coffee.

"Yes!" she replied to my message. "I'd love to get pho! But the next couple of weeks are really busy. Then I go home to California. When I get back, let's go out. Message me on the 1st or 2nd, I'll be back then ;)"

In the meantime I had others. A fuller-bodied North Dakotan by the name of Heidi who wore ironic sweaters and drank *Pabst Blue Ribbon*. She had overwhelming cleavage and plugs in her ears. We arranged a date. On the night of, she walked up that driveway in the suburbs, laughing, because she was so late, almost by an hour. She was the same as her pictures, good-looking in a wholesome way, despite the tattoos and piercings. We hugged hello and I drove her to a nearby bar, with its posters on the wall for the Vikings and Gophers and NASCAR. We drank our watery beers while the rest played trivia. We held hands.

"And if I get this next one right," I said, "we have to make out. I know, I know, but it's the way the system is set up." Heidi squeezed my hand. She leaned over. We kissed.

After our drinks we carefully made our way over the icy sidewalks past a store selling maternity wedding dresses. We stopped to joked about it and kissed again. At my car, I opened her passenger door.

"So fancy," she said as she got in. We went back using the side streets. "You know where you're going, fancy boy?"

"Don't worry," I said taking hold of her thigh. "We'll get there."

At the house, I gave her the tour, and though some have said things like "nice" and "homey" and "comfy," I wonder if Heidi and the others thought that place too middle-aged. Perhaps they thought I should've had a spot in a parking garage, a view of the river, and been within walking distance to cocktail bars. But Heidi seemed happy enough, lying in front of me on the couch as we watched a movie. Later, upstairs, we held one another. The lights on—we did not bother turning them off—our eyes closed, and it did not strike me as odd, as I appreciated the warmth of another body, that I didn't know this person, this Heidi. I couldn't say more than red hair, large breasts, works as a massage therapist. Maybe I was too oblivious. That's why I didn't notice her getting up.

"I'm good," she was saying, searching for her top. "I just have to go."

"But text me when you get back home, okay?"

"Okay," she said as she put on her clothes, the flesh of her hips sucked up by her tight jeans. Strapping her purse over her shoulder, Heidi went to the light switch. "You want me to turn this off?"

"Thank you," I said, and sleep fell on me like an ax. By morning, I had a message.

"This is embarrassing," Heidi wrote. "But I think I left my bra on your couch. Whoops! Can you pick it up for me?"

"Of course," I replied. I was at *Barnes & Noble*, browsing, when I passed a revolving wheel of children's stuffed animals. Heidi had a tattoo of an owl. There was a whole row of baby owls.

"Got a surprise for you," I texted as I walked out with it.

"A surprise?" she replied later that day.

Heidi and I were not in love, I knew that, but a red-haired massage therapist with large breasts, who would not want that for as long as they are given it? I texted about seeing a movie, and a day went by, then another, and another. On the fourth day I broke down and went to her profile. Heidi was online at that moment, and it hit me. I knew what I should have known days before, and as I absently scrolled through her pictures, I badly wanted to know why.

Not in generalities, either, I wanted specifics. My manhood, could that have been it? Or was it something more subtle? How I held my beer at the townie bar? My hair, did I have less than she imagined? Was my beard too long? Did I ask too many questions about who she had dated? Did I not ask enough? The way I smiled, was that not right? Did I pick a place for us to have beers that I shouldn't have, and did that forever turn her off? Was there something about the way I talked? Again, was it my hair?

As there were thoughts in the world, I had that many questions. And that is, I realized later, part of the reason why she didn't respond to me after our one night together. It's because she could sense I would exhaustively deconstruct why someone would want to kiss a person everywhere, then right after doing so, never want to again.

I gave up on Heidi and followed up with the one from California who did not play games. Jan, I still think. I emailed her as instructed, and after not hearing back for three days, a day after wondering every question with Heidi, I emailed Jan again.

"Jan! How are you? Have we missed our chance at online love forever? Our soup grows cold by the minute! Hope to hear from you soon, Robert"

It came as a shock, just an hour later, her reply. How it could have been, I do not know. It seems I am forever letting myself forget. This kind of thing cannot be dulled.

"Robert, hey," Jan—her name most likely—wrote. "I'm sorry, We're not on the same page. I'm not looking for someone who gets upset by this and you seem too eager to meet. I wish you good luck in finding what you're looking for. It's a crazy game, I've found, one that I'm still trying to figure out."

I never did write Jan to tell her she had reversed stances on online dating, that she had slipped and said it was a game. I think I was just glad for her. At least she was honest enough to admit it.

There was Kristin next, or KrisKris30, a bisexual Ph.D. student in Sociology at the University of Minnesota. I messaged her after she stalked my profile twice—the extent of work an attractive woman needs to put in at the website—centering my message around her picture where she pretended to push up a felled trunk in a Redwood forest. By the way she pushed—her legs squatted and her arms upraised—it seemed like she could be a fitness instructor. Over 30, no alarm bells went off, I only knew gratitude when Kristin responded back, assuaging my fading ego.

As I arrived at the pho restaurant on night of our date, she was already in a booth scrolling through her phone. When Kristin noticed me, she gave me a cunning smile, and we had a fine meal. Kristin told me a personal story about the time an ex proposed to her at a St. Paul Saints baseball game. She said "yes" that night, because she felt she had to in front of the crowd, but "no" later on. The story made her seem world-weary, which endeared me. I asked her about her last relationship with a woman.

"Nothing recently," she said, "but when I lived in D.C. I was with a woman a few times. I've never had a relationship with one, really. I just think they're amazing. They're put together well."

"I agree," I said, knocking my thigh against hers. She rested it against mine. We ate like that.

Our kiss came later, by her car. A slow, pleading thing, and after it was done she turned her eyes up at me, smiling in that way you do after you've been kissed. And though it all seemed real, as I watched Kristen drive away, I did wonder if we would see each other again. I had, by then, begun to doubt.

Persistence is maybe all it takes, because the next thing I knew I was sitting on her couch one sunny afternoon. A grown-up apartment in South Minneapolis with bookcases of academic books and exposed brick. Clean and put together, like it held literature readings for friends. Kristin and I watched a very boring science fiction television show, but what did that matter? We were on the loveseat in one of the spare rooms—one just for her cats to play—and we were on top of each other.

Later on her large bed, the windows let in light, Kristen was prone as I ran my hands down her back, and I asked about the few moles, one tattoo. She told their stories as I marveled at her pertness; her body reminded me of a gymnast's. After once more, we dressed, and at her doorstep saying goodbye— Kristin wearing only a t-shirt—I had a calmness in my belly. I saw ahead of me an afternoon of eating, watching football, the sun outside and the snow on the ground, as a man.

The next day, with that heady trot to my step, I texted Kristen about us going out to dinner, so we could have "a real date." A day after that, Kristen replied to say, "Robert, hey, I'm sorry. I'm busy that night. And you know I think you're really amazing and wonderful, but I just don't have time for anything right now. Good luck."

It may seem abrupt, but Kristen's goodbye was as good of a lie I could have hoped for; what would I have wanted? For her to outline my faults? Still I had to wonder. How often is it that we call the ones we never want to see again the most amazing and wonderful people in the world?

CHAPTER TWENTY

She grew up in Oklahoma and went by Dakota in real life, though I first knew her by NativeGurl22. Brand new to the website, NativeGurl22 seemed like a celebrity, showing off her hairy armpits and a butterfly tattoo spanning her chest, just above her breasts. She had bounds of black hair and tortoise shell glasses. Serious yet playful, she listed the poetry of Bell Hooks and the writings of Howard Zinn and said she spent a lot of time thinking about "sex, in all its glorious forms," and at the very end of her profile mentioned that one could not be "homophobic, racist, or classist in any way" if they wanted to be with her.

I sent a message, sure we would not go south if we met. Under the principle that an invisible justice kept the universe in balance, it seemed plausible to assume my luck would have to turn. In my message, I focused on NativeGurl22's dress, a tube-top flaring out at her waist with little crinkles, like something someone would have worn at Woodstock in the sixties.

"Why thank you," Dakota wrote back. "It's home-made." And she gave a smiley face.

Not an hour later, I had a number, and by the next evening Dakota texted me as she drank red wine with her friends. A girl who did not shave her armpits, who believed in sexuality as a spectrum and gender as a concept, could be mine. I was in bed in the suburbs when I got her text. Though I have to admit, when my phone first lit up, I hoped it would be Amariah. I did that for months.

"Oklahoma," it said, referencing our online chat the night before discussing home states. She was one half Native American.

"Dakota," I wrote back and soon there was another message, a picture. I saw the white collar of a dress, like from a Hutterite colony, and her hair so full it filled the screen.

"Now you," she wrote.

I got out of bed and had the brief thought of taking a shower, if that could somehow make me younger and have better hair. I stayed in my attic and put on my most modern of outfits: jeans, a paisley-patterned, collared shirt with a gray sweatshirt over that, and chukkas not tennis shoes. I angled my flip phone and posed my body in the stand up mirror in such a way to make me seem as if I were fit, as fit as I could be.

"Where's my picture," she texted, and I sent it. "Closer," she wrote. So I sent another, and she responded with, "Hmm, can't tell."

I fell on my mattress. I could send a million pictures. No matter how well they were taken, they would never be right. So, like an elderly person, I called. I didn't expect Dakota to answer, but she did, and what I liked most was her laugh, spontaneous and warm, the kind you might hear in church or a bar or in class and wish it was from someone you call your own.

And yet, in the days that followed, I couldn't help it, I sensed Dakota evaluating what I had sent her. In the shack of a hippie commune she must have lived in, I saw her swiping back and through between the two, contemplating whether I could be introduced to her rebellious friends, those who rode bikes with seats high up in the air. Somehow, we arranged to go out for pho.

"Alright," she texted in acquiescence. "But I am NOT going to shave my legs."

That was fine, but, on the day of, Dakota canceled at the last minute, saying she had to pick up a double at the vegan restaurant where she worked. The next night I found her online, and we began to chat, peacefully flirting, until I brought up the canceled date.

"You didn't believe me?" she typed.

"I do. I just don't normally do this much talking before I meet someone, usually."

"I do," she wrote.

"You do?" I wrote, then there was a good minute of nothing.

"Robert," appeared on my screen, then a break before the words, "don't press."

"Press?" I replied immediately.

"You're begging and that's not attractive."

"Less time on the internet," I sent, "that's a good thing…right?"

"True." And for a second I thought I had won her back. "But it's just," she continued. "I'm not sure. You seem great, Robert, but I don't like going on dates with people I'm not sure I'm totally attracted to."

I could never convince NativeGurl22, or anyone else, to want me. No matter how many times we talked over the phone, no matter how many witty things I said over a computer, no matter how many garbage cans I raided for the best day-old bread, her heart would decide. I could never employ a lawyer to sway it. For several minutes I typed and retyped my response, but nothing seemed right. Weeks later, I did text Dakota. I asked if she had found anyone who she was "totally attracted to." It seems, looking back, my worst moments have been in the time of online dating.

After Dakota, there was Kate, or SmallieBig. Spread over a blanket of time, I can't remember the website without her. She was there on the day I started, and is probably still there. In one of her pictures she held a baby goat, in another she was with her friends all scrunched in the back of a car, and the last one she danced in a room by herself, maybe on a night of drinking wine with her roommate. She was always there, but Kate did not belong on the website. I would be proud to tell others I am married to an Amariah, or a Kristen, or a Hannah, but every so often someone on the website will make you stop and ask, "What is *she* doing here?" Kate had straight hair and the body of a dancer. Her face reminded me a movie star from the 80s. We texted back and forth, one of our threads involving her playing *Dungeons and Dragons* with her friends as a stripping game. I prayed that someday I could join them. We made plans to meet at a bar called The Nomad.

A day before we were to see each other, Kate stopped returning my texts. I pretended that didn't matter by sending a text the morning of, asking what time was our date. Throughout the day, I babysat my phone. In the evening I sent another, and it was greeted with more silence. Days later, I sent Kate an email, asking why we never met up. I did not think I would receive a response. So I did.

"Rob, hey," Kate replied. "I'm sorry to hear about your unlucky streak. If it helps, I don't really see why you're going through that. You seem like a catch. That being said, I'm not really interested in meeting up. I have a hookup situation with a few friends and I'm liking it a lot. I'm sorry if I led you on by keeping this up here, I'm just keeping it up due to a gross combination of laziness and self-esteem biz. Anyway, again, I'm sorry about your bad internet dating luck, but I'm sure it'll turn around!"

CHAPTER TWENTY-ONE

B elieving Kate, I messaged Marie, a curly-haired yoga instructor. "Finally," Marie replied to me on a Friday night, "someone who can write…"

I was on the couch in the suburbs as I read her words. My week of work done, pleasurable things surrounding me, I thought again of the possibility of love. Saturated in pizza and wine, I wrote my second message to Marie. Later that same night, we were on the phone.

"Thing is," Marie said. Her voice was petite but not frail. "I've pretty much gotten to the point where it's impossible to meet anyone great on that website. I either meet really nice guys who aren't interesting or really interesting guys who are just crazy."

From her pictures, I knew Marie had a cropped mop of hair, a Hollywood kind of smile, and the body of a yoga instructor. "Ugh, my butt," she told me later. "It's kind of a thing."

"You've never seen my butt," I said. "It really is something."

"Barfing everywhere," Marie said, which she meant as a joke. We talked of traveling too.

"I'm planning a trip to Spain," I said. "I dabble in the arts. I'm a renaissance man, Marie. A revivalist of the lost art of living well. La Bella Figura, as they say."

"I actually haven't even been to Europe," she said. "What kind of loser am I?"

"Total loser," I said.

"Watch it, internet boy." And I could see Marie smiling through the phone. Lying back on her bed, wearing underwear that hardly even hope to cover her ass. Her legs doing some contortion, she played with her hair as she considered someone from the internet.

At the end of our talk, Marie told me about her last boyfriend. They had lived on a farm in Wisconsin and he was a recovering alcoholic. "Which is why," Marie said, "I stay away from any boy who has pictures of himself drinking. Well, unless he's super hot."

I was not super hot, I knew that, but as I fell asleep that night I did so with a grin, thinking of our possible future. I imagined Marie did as well. By the time I woke I had a text about how Marie was still "barfing everywhere," and it made me sure we would have some version of that future. The plan was for Marie to return early from her getaway in Wisconsin to have pizza with me in the suburbs. It was an old school place, not a chain, and that Thursday at work—watching medicine bottles go by—I was packed up and ready to leave the online dating world.

"So I was talking with my friends," Marie texted me in the afternoon. "They think it's weird I'm going to cut out to spend time with some guy from the internet. Hold for instructions."

"Holding," I wrote back like a coward.

"Alright," she sent minutes later. "I can't hang out this weekend. I'm staying in Wisconsin."

As a defense, I did my best to pretend it was all a game, like a woman from California named Jan, I think, once told me. "I guess I'll have to call up my other girls," I replied, "see what they're doing."

Marie sent, "I suppose" hours later.

Something had gone terminally wrong. I was not chill enough for someone like Marie. Later that night, a message. "Okay, if you want we can do coffee next week. But that's about all I have time for."

I didn't wait to respond. All forces were conspiring against me. "What day works for you?" I texted, asking like an obedient child.

"Maybe Wednesday? I'd only have like a half hour."

"Sounds like a plan," I texted from the suburbs. "Call in a couple minutes to hammer out details?"

There was a delay before she hesitantly answered, "I guess?"

I heard the rings of her phone as I walked up the stairs to my attic, confused thinking of how things could turn badly so quickly. What happened? We had talked about her butt. She was going to come to the suburbs for pizza. In a way, I think, it was old broken hearts and weird guys on the internet and everything else, but it was also me working against me. When Marie picked up, it sounded like she regretted doing so.

"Marie!" I said and saw her patience—in the reverberations after saying her name—dissipating like a lifting fog. "How are you?"

"Why did you want to talk?" she said. She sounded petulant.

"Just to get our plans set," I said. "I'm not big on texting for that. Gets laborious, you know?"

"Like I said, I'm busy, Robert. I might have time Wednesday, if you still want to do that."

"Sure," I said and could tell Marie was no longer undressed on her bed, playing with her hair. Instead bundled up, her jaw clamped, there was only the fuzz of our connection. I thought about the date she relayed to me on our first night on the phone, with a man who told Marie at the end of the night, "well, if you're bored or something, we should hang out again."

"Bored," she'd told me. "Grow some fucking balls and ask me out like a man."

In the present moment, I broke the static. "You know," I said. "It's weird that we're weird. I though you hated the Minnesota nice, passive guys….right?"

"Rob, please, if you're going to get serious, I really don't think we have much more to talk about…"

"Sorry, no," I said. "I'm not. Let's just go for coffee. I think we'll have a good time."

"Fine, but I gotta go. I'll see you when I get back?"

"Sounds great, Marie, see you then."

She hung up first, and I lay there on my landlord's mattress up in my rented attic with my heart racing for reasons I did not understand. The next night, a Friday night, wiped from a week of work but content to lie on the couch and be lulled to sleep with pizza and wine and TV, I got the message.

"On second thought," she wrote. "I don't want to have coffee with you. Good luck finding whatever it is you're looking for."

And I feel for the one who read that, I do. He is me, after all, someone who would agonize over an idea of a person and not the person itself. But I feel more for whatever he is now, someone who still cannot get this toxic idea out of his head. I can't shake the notion: I lost something great that I never knew.

CHAPTER TWENTY-TWO

I had to move away from those who only wanted a temporary interlude. I needed someone serious. From her pictures, JewessJewels seemed liked one of those. She attended galas, expensive weddings and planned events. She worked for Target in their downtown office as a jewelry designer, and by the way she presented herself it seemed as if she should have been on a paid dating website, one where people take things more to heart. Or, it could be that's not true, I don't know. Maybe the people on those sites act the same way but complain more about how much they pay every month to not find love.

Either way, JewessJewels was high class, even if it was her funniest picture that drew me in. Slumped in a chair after a fancy night out, she wore that Groucho Marx disguise, black-rimmed glasses with the fake mustache. It made her seem interested in someone like me, as if she had a sense of levity when it came to the vagaries of life. She would understand why we end up where we do.

So I sent a message about pho, and a week later JewessJewels—her name was Michelle—replied with, "What's your favorite spot?" But on the night of, she sent the text, and this time it went, "Sorry Robert. Not feeling well. Could we reschedule?"

With that I knew we would never be right for each other. But I was weak and alone, so I replied with, "okay." Michelle did not answer for two days, but I needed to take a chance on her. Only by meeting someone could I be sure. So we set up a date, this time for Thai, since my pho place was not open on Wednesday. Arriving early, like I always do, I scanned the place. Since Hannah, I had not been back. Seasons had come and gone, and as I waited in the lobby, no flood of good memories returned. Instead a strange thankfulness filled my stomach. No matter how much I missed Hannah and the comfort she gave, we were not meant for each other. At that moment I knew that as well as I knew anything. Michelle soon got there, looking like her pictures, if a bit more plump, as is often the case. I stood up to greet her.

"Hey," I said, smiling to put us at ease, though maybe she never learned that social norm, I joked to my landlord later. Michelle only nodded.

"How are you?" I asked, and her non-smile turn into a frown. We stood there not talking.

I think Jesus must have come down from heaven, because our booth in the busy restaurant came free much sooner than it should have, and sitting down seemed to relax her, us. Michelle began talking. I can't remember her stopping.

"Jewelry Engineer," she called her position. She traveled 30 weeks of the year, had friends in New York who had been on the cable television matchmaker shows. Woody Allen's aunt and uncle, Michelle knew them and other NYC notables, some of whom I had not heard of but didn't say as much, fearing I would be even more of a hick to her. It didn't really matter, Michelle didn't ask more than three questions. After dinner, we parted on the sidewalk.

"Thanks for dinner," she said, hitting the crosswalk button repeatedly.

"No problem," I said, taking steps down a dark, residential street. "Maybe I'll see you again?" I actually thought it might get better. She was very attractive.

"Maybe," she said, still hitting the button, and I let myself turn. When I drove back to the corner, the stoplight had changed to green and Michelle was gone. Driving home, I thought about all my desperate attempts, and all others made by sad people, to fill a loneliness with something we know is not right, all because of that thin small chance polluting our brain like a dye. I marched forward on the same path, searching for someone, to have something we later deemed substantial.

I found one. Not wild or dramatic or even that ambitious, LibraryGurl stated her appreciation for books and beer and camping trips. Her arms toned, her smile delicate, in her main picture she held a cupcake, happy but also somehow sad to have the dainty confection. She seemed wholesome though not dowdy, someone a man could want not just for a night but a lifetime. It was why I was there, to find someone to accompany me for that long. In my first message I told LibraryGurl how unique she seemed to be, the kind of girl "you just don't see around here." It was a line, but I meant it.

She stalked my profile, though she did not respond. I assumed LibraryGurl had others. A week later, I emailed her again, going lighter this time, comparing her looks to that of Lake Bell, someone with whom she did share a passing resemblance. And while it did get LibraryGurl looking, it was just looking, nothing else. Then came the night of another pointless time with someone I don't remember, and when I got back to the suburbs, I messaged LibraryGurl again. A knot formed in my stomach as I went to sleep, but the morning, a message, alleviating all my sickness and doubt.

"Thank you, Robert, for the kind words. I feel bad for not responding to your messages. You seem like a sweet guy. In fact, my New Year's Resolution was to get myself out there more. So I'm up for pho. Tell me the time and the place and we'll go from here. Molly."

So direct and true, it was how I knew LibraryGurl would write a message: understated, not too flashy, no emoticons but full of healthy life, with a clear-headed nature I loved.

It snowed on the day I met Molly. She sat down across from me and rubbed her glasses clean of a fog. She had taken the bus from St. Paul. I apologized for that and more.

"I'm sorry I messaged you so many times." Our soups were in front of us. "I don't normally do that."

"That's okay," she said, her brown bangs over her gaunt face. She was skinnier than her pictures. Dark circles hung under her eyes, making it seem as if she had endured sadness. I wanted to give her every chance in the world.

"You kept looking at my profile," I said. "I thought I'd keep on trying, you know?"

"I don't go on many dates."

"I don't either," I said, lying. I ate some of my soup to cover it up. "So how many do you go on?"

"Not very many at all, like, maybe I've been on two."

"Oh wow, so like in a month, or a week? A month, that's not very much."

"No," Molly said, "I've been on two dates before this."

"So you're new to the site?"

"I've been on it for about two years." Molly then blithely ate some of her soup as I tried to understand what that meant. After, I paid and offered to drive her home. She accepted, though we did not speak as we walked to my car through the snowy parking lot.

"Do you like Beyonce?" I asked inside while turning up the stereo. "I've been listening to a lot of Beyonce lately."

"She's okay," Molly said nonplussed, and so I left the music at a low volume. Halfway back, since it was a long route, I asked again how she got to our date.

"I took a bus to the light rail, then another one took me to the restaurant."

"Wait," I said, my car sloshing up a slushy mix of salt and snow. "You took two buses and the light rail?"

"It wasn't a big deal," Molly said, in a way that ended the story. Looking forward, I thought about her beside me, someone who had met two others and been online dating for the same amount of years, someone who got the most animated over pho when we talked about a bookshelf she adopted at the local library. I began to think of my depression, whether it showed on all these dates and how much of a turn off that must be.

I woke to Molly calling out a turn. Soon it would be the part where we said goodbye. I hated the thought of a handshake. I wanted a hug, maybe a kiss, but that just seemed tragic. Molly worked at the used bookstore we were about to pass.

"Do guys ever ask you out when you're working? I mean, I bet that kind of thing happens."

"Not really," Molly said wistfully. "I always kind of thought that's what would happen. That someone would do that and we'd date. It's kind of why I never use the site."

Just a few more blocks, and I parked across the street. Before getting out, we had a side hug in my car, a perfunctory gesture. We said goodbye almost simultaneously.

Once back in the suburbs I began to write a text to thank Molly for a pleasant time. I planned on using that word, pleasant, when a text came in. Not a goodbye but a, "Thanks for pho, it was really good! Glad you got me to go out. These socks are practically folding themselves now!"

I had asked what she planned do that afternoon.

"Laundry," Molly said. "I have a bunch of socks to fold."

Sitting in the living room, my landlord on the computer, I watched as more snow came down outside. Out in the drifts, Molly was turning into the one I imagined, the one who was good to people but also fun and alive. Maybe, I thought as I had a beer and watched the snow fall, she was just shy. It was all this time only meeting two guys. She would need time.

We decided, after more texts, for me to come to her place, to make sandwiches and watch a movie. It was a plan as good. Anything could serve as a flint to make sparks. I was just reassured in knowing Molly would want to see me more than once. I had begun to fear that would never happen again.

I pulled up in the darkness to Molly's place on a Saturday, to her two-story brick building in St. Paul. It seemed impossible, but there I was in her studio. Molly smiled faintly as I checked out her studio. I saw a made bed with a white comforter, above it were Buddhist flags, then a loveseat facing a tiny TV across an expanse of wood floor, plastic crates of books, a table with nothing, a kitchen with everything immaculately put away, a desk with a computer plum center in the middle, the fridge with one postcard, a cat roaming around.

"I cleaned before you came," she said, as if in a creepy movie. Yet still I hoped we would drink and end up in bed and Molly would show off her body, which had no fat, and we would ease one another's pain. I prayed for that, for us to change everything about ourselves.

"So," I said. "We should go get some ingredients?"

"Okay," she said. So we left for the grocery store, and I marched out of her place instead of walked. Something to make her happy. She locked the door efficiently behind us.

It was cold and we talked very little on the way While shopping, I hoped, things would break. Molly had mentioned her love for sandwiches and getting the ingredients would brighten us. But, as we went through the aisles, she said nothing more than, "sure." On the way back we discussed camp in junior high, for her in Wisconsin. Justin Vernon had been her counselor.

"He'd bring his guitar in and play bedtime songs," Molly said.

I mimicked his singing voice, "Was it all like... *for Emma...forever ago?*'"

"Her name wasn't Emma," Molly said.

"Right," I said, trailing off, "I figured that." We were quiet the rest of the way.

At the apartment we made our sandwiches, and if there had been surgical gloves, I think, we would have worn them. Compared to Molly's, exact in its measurements, my sandwich looked as if a land mine exploded inside of it. With my shards, I went to the small couch while Molly ate at her desk, feeding her cat small bits.

I drank a beer as she drank water. Neither of us said a thing, not until I mounted up for a last hoorah.

"Bring that computer over here. I'll show you a video." So she did, but, halfway through, I could tell Molly did not like it.

"Weird," is what she said.

"You're right," I said and turned it off, though I thought its weirdness was what was supposed to make it funny.

We watched an episode of *Peep Show* next, a show I loved but she had never seen, and near the beginning my finger hit Molly's knee. I tried, though awkwardly, to knead her neck, but her posture did not change. She watched her cat as it played with one of the Buddhist flags above her bed. Molly did not owe me a thing, but as I heard her giggling at the cat—doing something generically feline—all the gratefulness I'd felt for letting me know that I wasn't so hideous and that it wasn't so impossible that one day I'd be happy with someone had vanished. I wanted to let her be alone with her cat. I would take my troubles elsewhere.

At her door, time for goodbye. I had the leftover bread and chips. "So," I said. "This was nice."

"Yes," Molly said, "thanks for coming."

"I shouldn't ask this." I badly wanted to know what she thought of me. It seemed as if she might have the key unlocking the reason for why everything had gone wrong with everyone else. It wouldn't hurt if Molly laid out my weaknesses, showed me where I needed to improve. I lifted up my groceries, but all I said was, "Sorry. Forget it."

Molly gave a quick smile and began to close her door. I turned and heard the click of the locks. Then, as I walked down her ill-lit hallway, I wondered what she thought she might find that night, or what I might find. To this day, I have no idea. Only thing I know for sure is that neither of us found it.

CHAPTER TWENTY-THREE

I logged on some forgetful night after Molly and saw short curly hair, fluffy and airy, like a baby's. The user did not smile or show her teeth. She seemed real in a seductive way, and first thing I did was imagine our wedding. Encased in a sea of black in one picture, she sat in her apartment on some easy afternoon with her face close to the camera, her head tilted as if questioning why I, or anyone else, would be looking at her. And the way she described herself was elusive, she said she was looking for "common ground." I sent a message to Gracedbased hoping to help her find that patch of land.

"You're funny," she replied, "What are *you* doing in a place like this?"

Before I thought of a response, I looked at Gracedbased once more. What would life would be like with her? Maybe I could work at the factory, supporting her through law school. Later, we would settle in the country and important figures would come to our parties. In our late 30s we would create a child who would grow up to be exceptionally bright. It seemed unreal, the idea of meeting her. And it was, I suppose, because I did not hear back after my reply. Every few days I went to her profile and wondered if I said something wrong. More days passed. I dated others, yes, but I was more interested in Grace's dark avatar, mysterious as her words.

Then, without notice, it was gone. Grace deleted her profile, and without any contact information, I would never get a chance to find out if she was everything I had ever hoped. The frizzy-haired beauty who would one day be a lawyer was gone. Tonya. Kristin. Andrea. Erica. Molly. Enid. Ling—names came and went, then it happened. Grace reappeared, adding a picture to her once dormant profile, showing off her slim, curved body. Late at night, I began to compose a message, but halfway through I stopped. What was the point? I went to bed kicking myself for being so naive. The next morning, a message.

"Fancy seeing you here..." she wrote, and in the space between those ellipses, I was found. We exchanged phone numbers and set up a date for a Tuesday night. That evening, showered and ready, excited like a boy before recess, I had a brand new message. I read as my stomach sank once more.

"Rob, I hate to do this, but I have too much to do. Can we reschedule for this weekend?"

As a nothing of a man, I messaged her as soon as I could, making sure to confirm that we could. "No problem," I wrote. "We'll see each other this weekend. No worries." And yet I knew that a hesitance, a built-in resistance comes after a cancellation, one I have never been strong enough to overcome. When Grace and I met that weekend, it was like I should have never worried.

Across from me and as unreal as a ghost, she wore a shirt displaying what God gave her. They made a buoyant crease and I noticed their movements as she laughed. Grace had the same wispy hair and long neck and androgynous face, as well as an endearing gap in between her two front teeth. I was positive, as I watched her smile, it would be last night for me on a dating website. We ate our soup.

"So," I said. We were talking about our pasts. "You were pretty Christian when you were younger too?"

"Yes," she spoke with a small lisp. "My family is still, but we don't talk about that kind of stuff. They know my stance."

"Me too," I said and looked up to see her calm and attractive. Eerily romantic, how our experiences echoed one another. Souls split apart but reunited by the internet. "So what are you up to after this?" It was Saturday night. "Any crazy lawyer parties?"

"I do have one, actually. It's going to be lame but my roommate will murder me if I don't go. Literally, murder me."

"I want you to stay alive, Grace. Though if you feel like living dangerously and skipping out, you're welcome to come over. We're having a small get together in the 'burbs. There will be alcohol and music, if you're into that kind of thing."

"Hmmm," Grace said. "I could be into that." And she smiled again, showing that gap in her teeth.

We walked to her car after I paid, stepping in unison through the parking lot as flakes of snow came down like pieces of confetti. Heaven threw me a party as I tasted her *ChapStick* and spearmint gum. Dear God, I repeated as I drove to the suburbs, thank you.

Back with my landlord, he and his friends were drinking, and there was a TV, but it was all men, and they were drinking beer and watching college football. So I was not disappointed Grace never came over that night; it would have been an odd scene. Still, I tried. With the help of my landlord, we crafted messages by easing, barely asking, never telling, always timely, never anxious. For an hour we did this, the climax of which came in the kitchen with me and my landlord while Grace was with her law students in a living room I would have to imagine has a "woody" quality and she revealed to me that she had driven her roommate and could not go anywhere. So I stopped, but later, in bed, I felt what I was about to do was a brave thing, though it may have been the dumbest thing. No one will ever be able to tell me. Whatever it was, Grace did answer.

"It was pretty fun," she was saying. "We played *Pictionary*. My roommate got druuunk."

"That's cool, and, you know, I was thinking tonight, if you couldn't tell by my very subtle texts, we should hang out this week. I mean, if you wanna do stuff."

"I like stuff," Grace said. I could she was still smiling. "But I am so busy this week, Robert. It's crazy. Could we do next Sunday?"

I had to be strict with myself to not ask for breakfast the next morning. "Great," I said. "I'll see you then."

"Perfect. Alright, Robert. It's bedtime for this girl. I'll see you soon."

"Goodnight, Grace," I said, and when I look back at those words, they seem as good as any. If they had been the last thing we said to each other, they would have been like her name.

The next morning, because of my recent attempts at online love and based on the advice of my landlord and the other men at the party who all had wives and long-term girlfriends, I decided not to focus on Grace. No longer would I treat someone with such a precise intensity that all they could do was try and wriggle out of it. So that Sunday morning, a sunny one, instead of texting the one I saw the night before, I messaged someone I had noticed before on the website.

She added another picture the night before. In her others, I had seen, she hid herself under formal dresses and winter coats. But in the new one she wore a t-shirt at a rock concert. Her hair sweaty, her face red, and by how formidable her chest seemed to be, one could almost feel like the wind had been knocked out them.

"Girl Talk!" I wrote to her. "I know those guys (that guy?). Was that a fun show? Looks like it was a hot one for sure!"

Not a minute later, a text, and with it came a rush of adrenaline. Had her Sunday suddenly opened up? I was so happy. I sat on my chair in front of my computer in the attic. As I read it, I slithered to the ground.

"You just messaged my roommate!" Was Grace's text.

"Ha!" I texted from the floor. "What did I say?"

"Just something about the concert she went to."

"What?" I furiously typed. "That's your roommate? Crazy. I messaged her because I saw she had a new picture!"

"Not a big deal, dude, just thought it was funny."
And it was. We would have a good laugh at our 10th-anniversary dinner. What a hoot it would be then. I cannot say when I got up from my floor. I looked at the pointed attic ceiling for a very long time.

That afternoon was playoff football. I sat in front of TV by my landlord, but I didn't watch. I gripped my phone, staring into the empty spaces of time, minutes stretching into hours. I grasped it and willed for it to light up. But there was nothing for two days, not until Grace wrote me to say, "By the way, I cut my hair."

So I went to the website and saw that she had. Gone were the wispy curls, everything pushed forward and swirled up in a point. Grace also changed her profile, adding phrases I decoded as I had a drink at my computer in the attic.

"I'm looking for someone who's open and honest about what they want. I'm not into playing games and neither should you be."

Night drifted into morning. We had our date that Sunday, I still believed that, I think. And though my landlord admonished me to not, under any circumstances, contact her. I composed this message.

"Dear Grace," I wrote. "How about you and I run away together and eat pho and watch *Manhattan*. This busy workaday life is for the birds! Robert." I was kidding, maybe. I soon passed out.

"Rob," Grace wrote back sometime in the night. "That sounds lovely, but it's just not where I'm at right now."

At work that week during breaks, I held my phone. On drives home, whenever the traffic slowed, I crushed it in my hand. At night it was a struggle not to watch it like the ticking of a clock. On that Saturday, I acted like nothing had changed and asked where we'd meet the next day. On Sunday I did the same. On that afternoon I went to my computer. I knew of little else to do, and not a minute after I sent the poem, I had a text message.

"Robert," Grace wrote. "Don't you know we're all online because this whole thing is messy and terrible? I honestly don't think I'm the person you're looking for. I don't even think I know what I want, I just know it's going to take a while to figure it out. Good luck, Grace"

That was it, and it was nothing. If one could add it up, mine was a wasted collection of desires for another randomly wandering about the earth. As a rebuttal, I arranged for melodious notes to be sung. GoldDustWoman grew up in that wealthy first-ring suburb of Edina and received her undergraduate at the University of Minnesota. She was finishing her doctorate there when we meet. She had a face that did not remind me of failure. Everything about her was rejuvenating in a way I could not place.

"Recently," her profile read, "I went on a 'tunnel of love' kick (the bruce album, for sure). It's beautiful, just the best. So I'm hoping for a spring awakening."

GoldDustWoman had the most tranquil profile picture I had seen. Not out dancing, not bunched together with twenty of her friends, not trying to smile so hard it hurt, just good heart sounds went through me as she sat in her driver's seat. Looking over at the passenger, she smiled a relaxed smile. Her long and curly hair, almost red, tumbled over her forehead to her big brown glasses. I messaged GoldDustWoman, and she replied.

"That is so sweet," she wrote. "By far the best compliment I've gotten here. I was actually just taking my best friend back to my place from the airport when she took the picture. I hadn't seen her in almost a year and we were stuck in traffic. She caught a moment of pure love and joy. I'm glad you could sense it!"

I think a curse comes with detecting nuances like that. It makes one overly sensitive. But it can be helpful too, in this case it helped me recognize the goodness in a nearly red-haired woman working toward her doctorate in psychology, focusing on trauma and moral injury. I would be happy to see her. I would be happy at last.

If one was there that Sunday in Minneapolis, going inside a restaurant butting up against the Midtown Greenway on Nicollet on a spectacularly bright winter afternoon, they would have seen a man squinting from the brightness caused by the sun reflecting against the white snow. He was standing tall, wearing a black coat with a gold zipper. To a passerby, the jacket would not have been the most noticeable thing, but the beard, growing since someone had told the man he had gotten to be "too much, too soon." Reddish brown, untamed tufts contrast against his balding head. He wears jeans and brown leather boots and is checking his phone. He nods when people walk in.

I nodded to another, then saw her coming, and it was so bubbly, how Sheila (GoldDustWoman) walked, pushing up her glasses. She seemed in charge of herself, self-assured in a way that if she had fallen on the ice, she would have laughed and thanked the padding on her backside, which I saw shaped by a stretchy skirt as we walked in the place. Sheila wore slipper shoes and a gold cross of David and a low cut t-shirt. We ate.

"This is your first?" I asked. "Like first *first* internet date?"

"Can you tell?" she said and smiled again. On her profile she wrote the first thing people noticed about her was that. "Its breadth & frequency," she wrote.

"You're a natural," I said and took some noodles in the chopsticks. "What made you sign up?"

"New Year's Resolution," Sheila said. "I'd been on this long stretch of dating the same guys. Musician types."

"Ahh, band boys," I said. She was laughing as she took off her big glasses and wiped off their fog from the steamy soup. She agreed, saying she was done with them.

The rest of the date, I hinted at the sea of emotions without commenting directly on the torrents which would have scared Sheila away. Everything went so well. I even asked as we headed up to pay, "What're you up to now?" in a way I did not usually ask, not trying to superimpose my schedule onto hers.

"Headed over to my dad's house. He has really good beer and I have this trashy romance novel. You know, just veg out. Maybe watch a movie later. It will be glorious, Robert."

We were at the counter and Sheila rummaged in her purse. "It's okay," I said. "I got it." I think she appreciated that.

"So, a factory, huh," Sheila asked as we walked into the stunningly bright day. "My cousin worked in a factory in high school. Hard work?"

"It's not so bad," I said, and I don't remember saying another thing before we got to my car. We said goodbye.

"Thank you for a lovely first internet date." My shadow shielded Sheila from the sun as she looked up at me. Her eyes were open.

"Yeah," I said. "Let's do it again, I mean, not a first date, but...see each other."

I leaned back then forward, then back again. It was supposed to be a kiss, though we only hugged. But we had such easy chemistry, and since Sheila was doing nothing that day, I knew we would have a convivial back and forth of texting, that afternoon and probably the rest of our lives.

"Thanks for coming to pho," I texted from the suburbs. "Glad I could show you the ropes of the internet dating lifestyle!"

Though even as I hit send, I doubted. Not because of Sheila and I. We got along as well as two people could. Maybe I don't seem believable, but we did. I doubted because even if everything appeared perfect, there is always a second layer I am never able to detect. I didn't see it then.

By the early evening, I sat paralyzed by my phone. It became my only friend and my worst enemy as it became dark. We had only the lamp light, my landlord on the couch playing online games, his cat on his lap. And at last, my phone lit up. Her words are my water and my air.

"Robert," Sheila texted. "Thanks for the pho. You were a great guy to meet for my first internet date. I bet they can't all be this nice!"

I responded right away. "But they can be. Just stick with me! What are you up to this week?"

I waited for hours. Then days. And as more time went on, the crushing sense of being right about that invisible layer became too much. I did not write a poem, but I did write a message, and somewhere near the end, I wrote, "I thought we had such a good time." A month later, Sheila replied.

"Hi Robert. I wanted to tell you I did have a great time. You're a very sweet guy and definitely eased my way into this whole internet dating thing. I don't think I could have asked for a better IRL first experience. Unfortunately, I don't see anything further between us. Good luck, Sheila."

And I appreciated that, in a way, Sheila did not try to heal my perceived wounds with an exclamation mark, feigning to care as much as my mother or a best friend that I would find love. But at the time of its arrival, I had forgotten about her enough. I say enough because I still think of Sheila and her long curly hair and chic yet urban casual outfit and paralyzing smile. I had forgotten about her enough I didn't have my phone at the ready for her call. But I had to put up my best fight.

"Sheila," I wrote. She was still on the site. "I'm sorry, but I have to be honest, I don't know why you thought it was necessary to write me. If the roles were reversed, I have to believe you'd have found an email like yours pretty unwelcome. I'd be interested to hear your thoughts on us. Either way, next time, word of advice, if it's past a couple days, save the apologies. The silence is enough."

Sheila wrote back within the hour.

"Okay Robert, I'll tell you why I was not interested in seeing you again. First off, while it was a pleasant date, I felt like we talked too much about internet dating, which made it seem more like a meeting rather than something personal. As well, while I'm sure you're a nice guy, you struck me as someone a bit too wanting to be in a relationship, and that's not where I'm at right now. Lastly, and not to offend you, but I don't think I could be with a guy who works in a factory. That's not a personal attack, it's just my preference. Sorry if I upset you by not writing you back, it was not my intent. Again, good luck. Sheila."

That is how I remember GoldDustWoman, that and what she later added to her profile to explain to those who would like to message her: "If you'd like to go out for drinks or dinner, have charming and wide-ranging conversation, enjoy cleverness as an end unto itself—but not more than kindness—and are brave in matters of the heart and mind."

Brave in matters of the heart and mind. I once thought it was the only thing I ever was.

CHAPTER TWENTY-FOUR

I found a collage artist on the same day of Sheila's last email. And I thought, like Amariah, this is the one who is too much. I meant it in a way a husband tells his more beautiful wife, "what's a *dog* like me doing with an *angel* like you!" Hannah was the first. Amariah refined it. But Aleon, as she went online, was the manifestation. She had been made in a factory constructing attractive women with dense, curly hair and callipygian forms and artistic faces and larger, exceptional noses. Someone sculpted her. With the blueprint in hand, all I needed to do was send a message. I also had to ignore all the builder's recommendations.

Her age range, for one, stopped three years below my own, and she listed herself as being interested in "casual sex." In several of her pictures she wore sweats. It was a brazen fuck-all attack on anyone dumb enough to write her. So it must have been someone else who picked up my hands and machinated the keys for me that Sunday evening. Someone wanted to see me debase myself in every way. Aleon mentioned in the you-should-message-if portion of her profile that one should reach out to her if, "You don't want to get married right away."

I would have done so on the spot, but I said otherwise.

"Aleon," I wrote. "you're telling me you don't want to get married? That's unfortunate because I've got the rings, right here on my dresser. Let's see, the 24ct outlaid with baby diamonds mounted on a gold band, that's for my sorority sisters. Then the pearl ring with the wreath design, that one is for my mature ladies. We also have the conflict-free diamond for my social justice babies. I even have an assortment of ruby and topaz inlayed numbers for my tree-worshippers. Oh man, Aleon, I got so many rings. You have no idea. Shame you don't want to get married…"

Aleon replied with, "I'm kind of speechless. This is good….just…"

"Speechless," I wrote back. "That's too bad. Let's find your voice over pho this week. By the way, I want to call you Leon. You don't look like a Leon, but you seem like one. Does that make sense?"

"Omg," she replied. "My best girlfriends call me Leon. You're not a stalker, are you? If not, we need to go for pho. Well done, sir."

And so Leon, who was born Adamina, sat across from me. We ate soup. "Mine are a little better than most, I think. I hope, at least."

"A little?" Adamina said. She was speaking words to me. That was unreal. "Your message was way better. I feel sorry for most guys. The chance is either right away or never."

"Absolutely," I said, as if I would disagree. "I don't wait around. Usually by the second message, I go for it. That's why we're on the website, right?"

Adamina slurped up a hunk of noodles. She could have dunked her whole head in the bowl and it would not have looked bad on her. She was not kidding when she said, "I'd go out with a guy who asked me out in the first message. I don't want to spend more time on the internet than I have to. It seems like people on that site do."

"Absolutely," I said in disbelief. She echoed my sentiments. "And, you know, I was going to ask. I mean… unless it's too personal."

"Shoot," she said, confident in every word.

"Casual sex. Usually, people who look like you don't put down that they're looking for casual sex." I told myself not to do that, to allude to her attractiveness. But it was done.

"I dunno know," Adamina said. "I just got on it when I moved to Minneapolis last fall. I didn't want to date anyone, but I still wanted to have fun, or whatever. But you're right, I'll probably take that part down. I might take the whole thing down. It's really not worth it."

"At all," I said, as if I had never fallen for anyone and sent them poems and been unable to do anything—not sleep or eat—because they did not reply to one of my texts. We ate our soup. Later, after I paid, we walked out at night and came upon her car with Connecticut license plates.

"This is me," she said, so I peered inside. "Don't, please, I haven't cleaned it." She took a hold of my arm. I tried to conspicuously flex.

"Nice," I said, noticing an assortment on her middle console. "Still going with the tapes."

"My car isn't very 'advanced.'" And we locked eyes. "Thanks for the pho," she said. "You're a pretty nice to guy hang out with." Adamina slugged my shoulder.

"You're not too bad either, Leon. So you're going bowling now?"

"I'm already kinda late. But we should hang out again, bub."

"Definitely," I said. Our farewell loomed. I went in at her like a hungry bird, but thankfully and gracefully—as she must have learned from others— Adamina glanced out of it. We embraced, and after it was over I opened her door. From inside her car she gave me a small wave and drove away. By the time I got home, I had a text.

"Just got a strike. I think you're good luck."

It was her unprovoked goodwill that I used as inspiration. I poured a glass of water instead of a glass of vodka and went up to my attic. My room was a mess, so I cleaned. I cleaned and cleaned, and when that was done everything else seemed easy. I had job applications, which I unearthed under a pile, and filled those out. I did push ups and sits up. Exhausted and exhilarated, I went to sleep like a child, without an alcoholic lullaby. Thoughts of Adamina filled my head. I was so grateful for everything.

We texted throughout the week. Adamina worked at a daycare and sent updates on the kids, a lazy co-worker, a picture of a sandwich she ate, things you tell a new person in your life. I went down the stream her life-giving waters fed, feeling the sun on my back. On a Thursday evening we dined at a restaurant requiring reservations. Sitting down in the classy booth, surrounded by tables of middle-class yuppies—those with jobs in marketing and Minnesota public radio—I was brought back to Hannah again. Circling my water glass, wearing my best outfit, I wondered if she ever thought of me. That disappeared as Adamina walked in, and the way she looked, more attractive than anyone else in the place, made me jittery enough that when she came over I got stuck between sitting and standing, so I did a kind of jig. We somehow managed a side hug.

"Hey," she said as she sat down.

"Hey," I said, "you look nice." And Adamina did. She told me over pho she never dressed up, but she wore a fashionable scarf that night and black skirt and leather shoes, with laces up to her ankles. And makeup, she wore dark eyeliner and red lipstick, she would not wear these things for just anyone.

Adamina drank a glass of wine and I had a beer, and I should admit, what began as a fear over soup was confirmed as we waited for our food. She could only talk of herself, though I cannot blame her for that, good-looking as she was. Our most interesting conversation came as we went over the signals Adamina's friends and her used to describe hand jobs. After looking over her shoulder to make sure no one eavesdropped on us, she recreated the motion.

"Kinda like this," Adamina said, twisting and bending her fist, leaving a hole the size of a sausage. "Me and my roommate do it all the time. It's our secret handshake."

"That's a fancy one," I said

"It is, isn't it? But we have even fancier one…"

"Do you? What does that look like?"

"I can't show you here, but one of my friends tell me I have DSL." And her lips were beautiful, distended like they had been bitten by something poisonous. "You know what that is, DSL?"

"Maybe," I said. "But how do you know such things?"

"I didn't, really, not until they told me."

"I'll just say no comment." I said that because I was trying to think ahead. Those kinds of topics, I'm sure, are fine for some, but they are never okay for someone like myself, as they seem to get me, and whomever I'm with, to a place where we do not belong, past where a heart is safe, exposed like in a desert where one can only survive with the aid of another. I didn't tell Adamina that. I just kept listening to every word that fell from her stupidly plump lips.

After I paid, we walked across the street from the restaurant, and for once I had parked close. There was something I needed to give her. A busy street behind us, it was peaceful inside my car.

"These are for you," I said, handing her a plastic grocery bag with three jars of sweets she said on her profile she could not live without.

"Aww, Robert, this is so nice." Adamina leaned over, gave me a kiss as a thank you. Staying there a moment longer, we began with intent. To be tangled up in her was good, to run my hands through her so thick it was snarly hair, to have my hand by her flat belly, then her shaved everything, and to listen to her finish. My mind was clear as Adamina swallowed me in the cramped front seat. Lying back our on reclined seats, I brushed back her hair and kissed her neck.

"Thank you," she said. "Thank you. You're nice. Thank you." The car was heated. "Jesus," she said. "My ass is hot. How do I turn this down?"

"Whoops, sorry, I can do that." I reached over and turned down her seat warmer. We fell into each other once more.

Listening to the radio on the way home, oblivious to the possibility of anything ever going wrong, Adamina's affection blotted out my senses. By that Saturday, she consumed me. I knew she'd be doing little less other than maybe cutting and pasting as so to create more art. I began a conversation.

"Tomorrow," I texted from my landlord's red couch, "when you come over for our day of junk TV watching, what kind of snacks should I get?"

"Dude," she replied a few hours later.

"Adamina, this TV won't watch itself."

"True, that's true," she texted back. "Free tomorrow?"

It was what I needed. If Adamina would have me, I could be the interesting, good-looking person I had always imagined I would be. Of course I was free.

That Saturday night one of my landlord's college friends came over and we watched *Braveheart.* Both men both had girlfriends, but I was the better man. With the sun the next morning came the feeling of opening presents on Christmas morning. Though as our afternoon inched closer, the excitement drained, and in its place came the dread. I began to obsessively check my phone. Adamina would soon text me saying she would not be able to make it. Then, it finally came.

"Just looked up your address," said the text. "You live far away! Heading out in a few. See you soon."

I could have melted in the couch. Looking out through the windows on such a triumphant, clarion day, I tried to imprint its negative on my mind. To hold on to the fact that soon I would be with someone so attractive it hurt me to think of her. Not more than an hour later, I went out to greet Adamina as she emerged from her green 90s Volkswagen parked on the barren street in the suburbs. Instead she came down the driveway and excitedly ran toward me with a kiss and a warm hug. We held hands inside, quiet on a Sunday afternoon that felt like naps and football on TV. Adamina wore sweatpants that day, saggy and loose. We sat down on the couch and she flipped through the channels.

"I'd never leave the house if I had this big of a TV. Seriously, Robert."

Soon after that was the soft fabric of her sweats. Then her smooth legs, then we were climbing up the stairs, tripping over one another. Her figure. The way she smiled when undressed. It was her.

"Thank you," she said after. "You're so thoughtful. Do you want to sideways 69 too?"

"Of course," I said, and so we did. We did other things as well, and I was firm in knowing I did the best I ever could.

"Did that feel good," she asked after, stroking my hair, what was left of it. My head on her chest, just below my eyes were her perfect, ample breasts. I breathed out.

"Yes," I said as I kissed her neck. "Very much."

Resting by her crotch, I listened to her tell a story among her blue faded underwear. She talked in a vaguely Northeast accent about a friend of hers who made synthetic drugs at home. An hour could have gone by before we got dressed and went downstairs. It was dark out as we watched more TV and my landlord played his online game. Adamina was not shy. Our legs across the couch, we fit together like interlacing bricks. An hour or so after that her roommate texted because Adamina's roommate was young and attractive and they were best friends, and that is what they do, even when there is nothing to say. Adamina showed me the message.

"Why aren't you home! You have to be home whenever I need you!"

It included a picture of their cat and small TV. Adamina texted back a picture of the TV she was watching, and the cat my landlord had in the suburbs, as if she had found a new life. And I know, if I would've had one of those rings at that moment, I would have given it to her.

Adamina did not stay the night. By her car, near spring in the amber darkness, she reached up and gave me hug goodbye. I did not say a word. I did not ask if we would see each other again. Doing so would have soured a flawless afternoon. She drove away.

"How's movie and Chinese food night?" I texted later that night. Adamina and her art friends watched a movie and had Chinese food every Sunday night.

The next afternoon, after not yet hearing a reply, I asked Adamina out to see a movie. In the text she eventually sent, she used the phrase "too relationshipy," and asked, perhaps rhetorically, if relationshipy was even a word.

I never offered my opinion.

CHAPTER TWENTY-FIVE

L ong after I should have, I deleted my profile. Doing
so gave me such a purifying feeling I put in my two
weeks at the factory. On my last day, I was given a half-
hearted party in the break room—a small cake, two
cards, stale chips—and when it was done I cleaned out
my locker and left with no job or prospects. A man over
30 living in the attic of another man's house without a
wife; it was worse than that, a man over 30 living in the
attic of another man's house without the kind of life a
wife would want to enter. At least I found another job
quickly.

I believed it would be a step in the right direction.
Close enough to that house in the suburbs, I could walk
to the bookstore and save money on gas. I understood,

even then, retail for anyone outside of high school or college is considered unseemly, but I didn't care. I would be around people who loved the things I loved: books and movies and music. No longer would I feign to understand the life of someone who worked at a job because they had to work at a job. But it was all a sham. There was nothing artistic about it. The bookstore was part of a chain company and next door to a store in a mall that sold housewares.

Very soon after I started at the bookstore, I got an itch to reinstate my profile. One night, fighting the urge to do just that, I saw online a poster for the poetry and fiction open mic at an art museum on the University of Minnesota campus. It would be put on by two sisters who ran a local blog. I started a new poem of my own.

We grow a garden
We tend goats
You wear a hat
I fix our tractor
We raise chickens
We sell your eggs

All poetry is unnecessary, in a way. It thrived in a time when beauty could only be expressed with words or paintings. Now there is *Vine* and *Snapchat* and *Tinder*, and there are things, ten years from now, which will make those things seem quaint. Ten years from that, the same for what replaced them.

At the time of the open-mic night, I still had hope that one of my poems would get noticed and I would become an artist. After getting tenure and having a few books published, I would attract devoted esthetes who looked up to me for knowledge. With that vision, I finished my poem for the open mic, describing the ups and downs of being an love with an artist.

A cold night in Minneapolis, sharply so, on the night of reading. I got there early and signed up then went to the gift shop and absentmindedly browsed art books. Alone, expect for the cashier who studied.

"In 10 minutes," I heard over the intercom, "in 10 minutes we will have a tour. Please join us."

The museum has a view of the water and downtown, and as I waited I became more intimidated by the people I saw milling around out in the main area. Only the thought of becoming someone who never would online date again kept the crumpled-up piece of paper with a poem in my pocket. Later, just as the first person read her work—an older woman mewing about trees and wind—my landlord showed up. He gave me a thumbs up as my name was called.

Up on stage, the lights were brighter than I expected them to be, the microphone more imposing. The
meeting room was more full of artists, and it was much
too quiet. Everyone had been given a fake introduction,
so one of the sisters running the event said, "Robert
once threw a baseball so high in the air, it never came
down."

I tried to laugh, wiped my mouth and began, and if
anyone liked what I read, I don't know. I hope someone
felt something. Maybe a true thought was translated.

"That was really good," my landlord said as I sat down.
"Really, the best one."

There was one more, the one right after me. Hot
is the best word I can use for her, and as she read I
wondered what she thought of my work. If it was good
enough for her to consider marrying me. I think her
story was about a slab of meat and its place in the future. I don't know, it was nonsense, that didn't matter. It
seemed as though her words came out of her mouth as
notes. She had long brown bangs, a red mouth, one taking up too much of her face. I wanted to get used to everything about her. I would never get the chance. Soon
as she was done, instead of walking back to her seat, she
strode out of the hall, and I watched her go. I watched
my wife leave without ever meeting her.

After the final thank you for coming, my landlord and I left too. At the front door we discussed where we should go to celebrate. As we did, one of audience members padded my shoulder just before he escaped into the frigid night.

"I really liked your poem," he said and kept walking.

Amazing what a compliment can do. They can make a man think, at least for a short time, he might be on the right path. I was among culture at the bookstore in the suburbs and I would be a poet. I told no one at work about my other life. I let them—the part-time senior citizens, the chirpy managers, college students on break—live in ignorance as they brushed against greatness. I began to buy and study books for the GRE. A master's degree would be my next step in life. Also, I reinstated my dating profile. Holding off for almost two months seemed like a long time. Showers of possibilities awaited me, and I joined with new pictures, again taken by my landlord, where I wore short jean shorts in the snow.

Abigailish, the online version of Abigail Kiener, would be the first I messaged with that new profile, a graduate student in the fiction writing program at the University of Minnesota. I wrote to her with the kind of confidence—albeit a wholly manufactured and fantastical kind—that comes when knowing what one should do with their life. A tomboy writer with dark eyes and black hair, like a raven, she seemed right. Her profile was cocky, I would say, and I am sure others who saw it would have agreed. She wrote that she had failed to find anyone as "intelligent and ambitious as they were happy in the Twin Cities."

For two years she had lived in Minneapolis without ever finding even one. She also said she did not want to be the entertainer of the couple, and she needed someone tall. She was demanding, and I admit I saw what she wrote as a warning flare, but only a far-off glowing ember. Its heat couldn't stop me. It hadn't before. So I sent a message, one I took an hour to compose. The main hook was grammatical. Perfect, I thought. Just perfect.

"I recently read that a semi-colon is as useful as a semi-boner. Disregarding the gauche nature of the above idea, I have to agree with its main thrust, if you will. Semi-colons are rather useless. But then I see someone like yourself using them, and I have to take pause; is the semi-colon better than I thought?"

Abigailish wrote back with an a bright and crackling thing, agreeing with me but adding that she liked things like semi-colons, especially dashes because, "My phrases—their sometimes long and diverse meanings— I must separate them!"

And soon we had a date. Summer encroached on the city, though it was cool, just past dinnertime, as I talked on the phone with a friend in Chicago while waiting for Abigail to arrive.

"I'm trying not to get my hopes up too high," I said, balancing myself on a concrete parking block behind the pho restaurant. "I mean, even if you think something like this is going well, it's possible it isn't and you don't even know it."

"What's her deal again?" my friend asked.

"She's a writer. Went to Yale and wrote *The New York Times*, that kind of thing."

"Wow, well good luck, man. Don't get twisted over just this one. A lot of 'em out there."

And I think I knew that as I said goodbye to my friend and walked in to get a table. I think I knew others in the world existed. But I lost I saw Abigail came in and exasperatedly fling her bag on the chair, her hair wildly straying in every direction, swiping her bangs across her forehead.

"Hi," she said, getting out a book and a notebook. She had a kind of light happiness that cannot be duplicated.

"Sorry I'm a little late...hi," she said again and shook my hand.

"Hi. Good to meet you..." I almost made a reference to a song by the Magnetic Fields, but did not, assuming she'd got that from other unoriginal guys before.

We had our pleasantries, and since Abigail was new to the site, we got into internet dating. I did well to remember her profile and did most of the talking. We ate our soup.

"So there was Amariah," I said. Then Adamina. Now Abigail."

"Jesus," Abigail said. "We've all got the same name."

"They were a bit younger, how old are you?"

"27. And honestly, Robert, I wouldn't recognize the person I was at 23. You should start skewing the other way. Us old maids aren't so bad." I had to stifle a laugh.

"You haven't met your internet prince?" I asked.

"Lol," she said. "No. Am I supposed to? I mean, I was with a guy from the site last fall for a hot minute. We went on dates, so I didn't go on any other dates. I thought that was what you were supposed to do? Turns out you're not. Anyway, he was crazy. Punched a hole in my wall."

"What?" I was incredulous, too much so.

"It wasn't that big of a deal. He was an alcoholic, but an interesting guy. He's the one who got me turned on to Lish." Abigail had a Gordon Lish novel on the table, along with a book on ancient Chinese history. "Though I should tell you about this guy from last week. This psychiatrist. We went out to eat and he had smart things to say but there wasn't a love match there. That was clear, I thought at least. But then this last weekend, at like one in the morning, he texted me and asked if I wanted to have emotionless sex, which I thought was a totally fucked up thing for a psychiatrist to say."

"It is," I said. "But, I don't know. Maybe he thought he could say that because he was a psychiatrist. Like, that's his line, to feign being able to avoid being emotional since he knows how to extract emotion from a situation."

Abigail grinned. She had a woman's body and wore a patterned dress. She looked like a modern day Sylvia Plath.

"So," she asked as she ate, "do you write?"

"Sometimes, I think, poetry. But I don't have an MFA. I don't know, sometimes, and no offense, but sometimes it seems like that degree is a diversion from writing. You know?"

"The MFA gig is a weird one, Rob, for sure. Still not sure why I did it, but I'm here now, so, you know, fuck it."

Abigail was as her profile, and I enjoyed meeting her as much as I enjoyed meeting anyone. We finished our soup as we talked on the specifics of why she joined the site. I didn't think of bad things happening. I never do.

"All the guys in my program are a no-go," she said. "They're either married or too caught up with the undergrads. I'm open to love, whatever that is. I like to think I'll be in it again."

"Those dudes in your program are idiots, Abigail." And I meant it. Before we left, I told her I worked at a bookstore. We were outside, our steps matching. Abigail was tall beside me.

"Bookstore," she said, "that's the kind of job I need. Low stress, right? You should hook me up."

"I could do that," I said. "Of course, yeah, I could do that." But when I said it a second time, I trailed off. I think I was trying to apologize for not having a more distinguished career. In some way, we needed to acknowledge the facts.

Nighttime, and on one side of us were cars parked on the street and bicycles parked in metal racks. On the other, we passed ethnic restaurants. Abigail was smirking. It seemed she did that the whole time. Nearby at a coffee shop, where she planned to study that evening, we said goodbye.

"Thanks for the pho," she said. "Have a wonderful rest of the night, Robert."

"I'll call you, okay?"

"Okay," Abigail said, and reached out for a hug.

I went home hopeful but didn't hear from her after two separate texts, so I emailed, wondering what happened. Nothing for three weeks. Then it came, her reply, and there is one word from Abigail's email that sticks out, a word I cannot seem to get out of my mind.

"Yearning," she wrote as my sin. It was then. It is still.

CHAPTER TWENTY-SIX

I recently read that if you see two people kissing passionately in public assume these are two people from the internet trying to force something that isn't there. Reading this speculation made me think more critically about myself and what once did as an online dater. All the while, when I thought I had found something real with every new one I met, it was just a strategy by myself, or by her, to impart meaning into a time we did not want to later look back on as nothing. We had to try and convince ourselves that the days, months, years even, spent on that website had meant something.

I didn't believe that then. So I messaged another who said she was "shy at first but outspoken later on. Logical, but very emotional. Sweet but crass. Laid back

but organized. Romantic but sarcastic. Open but guard-
ed." She worked in a corporate setting and said, "it's
kind of ridiculous how much I get paid to do so little."

JessWeathers was a mass of contradictions and enjoyed the writings of Lydia Davis and Donald Barthelme.
She had an artfulness about her. Her photos were moody
things: black and white, pursing her lips, with such sad
eyes, as if she was about to cry or had just finished. So I
messaged her. And she wrote me back. We met at a bar.
How unique.

Sitting across from each other in a noisy place on a
Friday night, the waiters and waitresses, with colorful
tattoos on their arms, scurried by with circular trays of
organic beers and gluten-free fried calamari. I looked
at Jessica, it was her name, and wondered if she was less
or more attractive than her pictures. Her head seemed
small for her body and she had a drooping bosom, and
when she smiled, she contorted her mouth. But when
she laughed and touched her hair, another version of
her appeared, and I was taken. Jessica wore a dress—
purple and silky and not so hip—and we talked about
her office job, her favorite band the Black Keys, and
her undergraduate college life at Iowa. We could be
something, even only for a short time. After the drinks
and appetizers, I drove Jessica back to her downtown

apartment building. In our seats, neither of us moving for the door or for each other, we waited for the goodbye.

"Thanks for the ride," she said. Her name was Jessica, I have to remember that.

"No problem," I said. "Let's hang out again." How many times have I said that, I thought for a second. I wondered if my requests had started to sound artificial, no matter how much I meant them.

"Definitely," she said. "This was nice." I noticed her eyes were green. "Thanks again," she said as she got out of the car. We had not touched. We did not even hug, and as I watched her open the door to her building, I was positive I would never see her again.

I went on another date that week with a liberal Christian. I thought I could convert her, or she thought she could convert me. Whatever it was, OhMeOhLife and I traded emails after I began with a question.

"Miss OhMeOhLife, if I could ask, what do you think was the point of Jesus' death if there's more than one way to get to heaven? If He was tortured and killed and rose three days later for the sins of the entire world, wouldn't it negate that sacrifice? If we can go through another person and still make it into heaven, what's the point?"

An audacious question, I know, but if one day we fell in love, we would've had to say it was right. OhMeOhLife, in her pictures, was out swing dancing and showed off her healthy breasts, sandy blond hair with a small curl at the bottom, just past her shoulders. She eluded my question by responding with, "I have my worldview that informs my relationship with Christ, I wouldn't want to impose that on anyone else."

It was a clear sign, but I needed someone. So we met at a bar like any other, with tables, not booths, all dark except for candles, and most everyone there was dressed well. OhMeOhLife, or Ruth, pedaled up by bicycle, as nice-looking as her pictures. She wore a top that show-cased what God had bountifully given her.

"Nice basket," I said as she locked her bike to a post. She looked up at me.

"You're tall," she said.

"Blame my parents," I said. We laughed, I think. We walked inside. Across from me, Ruth drinking her second drink as we talked about premarital sex. That's what some call it. I once did.

"I've been with two guys," Ruth said. "But they were both my boyfriends at the time. I'm not against casual sex, it's just not for me. I don't think it's a sin or whatever."

"Really?" I said, perplexed. "Doesn't Jesus say that even looking at someone with lust is worthy of hell?"

"He says that?" Ruth grinned, and took another drink.

"I think he might? But hey, if you're willing to look past the stuff that prohibits sex, I can't blame you. I'd ignore all the parts of a book that didn't let me have fun too."

"Don't take it all so literally, Robert. There's a lot of beauty in the Bible."

"A lot of ugliness too."

"Ugliness?" Ruth said. "No, there are so many meaningful passages, so many."

"Alright, but you know the Bible was written around the time of the Iron Age, and those people didn't know the world was round. It's like what Albert Einstein said." I did my best James Bond and took a drink.

"Go on," Ruth said, her smile not disguised by the rim of her glass.

"He said, I think, something like, 'the Bible is an honorable but purely primitive book of childish legends.'" I was trying to seem more intelligent than ornery, like I couldn't help but expunge those sorts of quotes from my body. Ruth interrupted my insincere portrait.

"But Einstein believed in God, didn't he?" As an answer, I raised my glass, and Ruth raised hers. By the time our check came, we were both buzzed. We walked to her place to play video games. A flimsy premise, it's true; I thought about how I would soon be lost in her giant Christian breasts.

At her place, Ruth turned on the video game. We didn't have any drinks and her roommate was knitting in the kitchen for a good while. It got very late.

"I don't think my eyes can look at Mario anymore." She had taken off her top. It sat on the floor along with the most impossible of sheer camisoles. Her bra was red, the color of the blood going through our veins.

"Okay," I said, and got up. We went to her door.

"You're tall," she said again, and we kissed. Things got heated enough I nearly unhooked her garment, one that had been charged with an impossible task. But I think Ruth could sense what was happening, and no matter what she said in the bar, her actions were guided by a more chaste directive. She pulled away, put her hand on my chest, and said, "Goodnight, Robert."

"Goodnight," I said, and she closed the door.

The next day, Ruth sent me a message detailing the reasons for why we could not be together again. And I appreciated that, that she would take the time to write someone she only met once. It helped soften the blow of knowing I would never see her breasts. If God did exist, He would make things such as those. It was Saturday night when I read the email and I planned to drink and message past failures in the form of another poem. Right before I began, a text message came in at almost ten at night. It was Jessica from the week before.

"Hey," it said. "What are you up to?"

I had sent her two texts and both had gone unanswered. "Not much," I hastily replied while trying to make it seem as if her message was no big deal and did not feel like it came out of left field. "You?"

"Just seeing what you were doing."

I figured I may as well offer everything. "Did you want to come over and have a beer, watch a movie?"

"Sure," she sent. "I don't have a car, though. What's your address?"

My address, the suburbs, I sent it anyway.

"Oookay," she replied. "It's kinda far. I'll take a cab. See you in about an hour?"

Like that, the one who would be a footnote could be a chapter, at least. When I saw the cab arrive in the suburbs, I walked out into the night to pay the driver.

"You don't have to do that," Jessica said as she gathered up her purse in the backseat.

"Don't worry about it, I got it." I gave the man the money. We did not dawdle on the street.

Inside, the landlord playing his online games again, Jessica and I sat on the loveseat. She talked with him about whatever, I didn't care, her leg was over my leg. My hand under her hand. Fortunes change.

"I need a smoke," she said after a bit. "Wanna come outside?"

"Sure," I said and trailed behind her. I looked back. My landlord winked.

On the back porch, Jessica told me how she got her well-paying office job. Her grandmother had a board position at the company.

"But it's definitely not what I'm doing the rest of my life," Jessica said. "I'd like to get my MFA. I want to write." She took a long drag from her cigarette.

"You should come up and read my poetry," I said. "Tell me what you think."

"We could that." And she gave me a nod that comes when smoking a cigarette. We headed upstairs. Jessica on my lap as she read my poem.

"Any good?" I asked.

"Well...I don't know if I believe it. It's nice, I just don't know."

"It's a poem, Jessica, it's not supposed to be believable." Though I knew what she meant. I didn't care. I put my hands on her neck and kissed her. We went to the carpet, and I tasted her. We made our way to my bed and her breasts were impressive, but long, like she had borne children. She finished first, then I did. In the calm darkness after, I was glad to be next to her. That was short-lived.

"I should get going," I suddenly heard, and Jessica was getting out of bed. I reached for her hand, but she pulled away with more strength.

"Jessica, it's like three. I'll take you back in the morning."

"No," she said, sitting up. "I need to go. I'll call a cab. Go to sleep." She nudged her body off the mattress and onto the floor and began to find her clothes. I flopped my head on the pillow like a child and pushed the blanket off of myself. "What are you doing?"

"You can't wait by yourself," I said, which made her shoulders drop. For some reason I did not understand she wanted to be alone. But I couldn't allow it. As I looked for my shorts, I chided myself for ever trying to win the affections of another human being.

Shirtless on the couch downstairs, I tapped my foot as Jessica called for her ride. She sat two cushions away. "Twenty minutes," she said.

I said nothing, just nodded my head, and for the next half hour I heard her say, like the ticking of a clock, "I just need to sleep in my bed, it's nothing you did." Then she was gone.

I wrote Jessica the next day, worrying my penis had not been enough, that she had tabulated its width and length and thought better of confusing things. Leaving in the middle of the night would be an unmistakable ending. Though even as I worried, I knew that part of me was fine, or at least serviceable. I never overwhelm anyone with it, I know that, but it has never been a hindrance. It was what I realized later, when I didn't hear back from Jessica and she stayed on the site. That ours was not distinctly a case of forced passion, like so many other online daters—though it was some of that as well—ours was a case of mistaking the passion I gave as a doting love.

CHAPTER TWENTY-SEVEN

After Jessica there was Celia. She told me she was arrested when the Republican National Committee came to Minneapolis in 2008. Then Jenny, the artist who lived in the country. Then Veronica, the lawyer who wanted only phone sex. Then Anne, who showed me a picture of herself in a thong while we ate brunch. Then Sara, the round-assed Native who went to Yale and whose dad was a surgeon. Then Becca, who called herself a "Sad Little Muffin." I laid myself bare. I wanted bodies against my body without striving for something meaningful in the way we bummed up against each other. That was pointless.

The first worked at a department store and did great things with her mouth. The next one said she could make it clap, and I found just below her waist, in broad and detailed cursive, "Every day I'm Hustling." Then a tall woman who worked as a photographer and went on trips overseas and outdoor festivals by lakes. She was a mountain to climb.

Then another who said in her profile she hated pho and was blond with short cropped hair. In her profile she sat on a child's plastic slide holding a glass of wine and said, "take me anywhere," so I did, within physical limitations. After that someone from Iowa who worked as a hairdresser at the Mall of America and brought over fudge to the suburbs and had tattoos covering her body. Then the one who made cake pops and had a body like a basketball center and the hair on her head was streaked with blond highlights but nowhere else.

Then the one with an afro who I had seen so many times on that website and talked to me after we were done about her addict ex-boyfriends. Then another who came over with her dog. She had silky blonde hair and worked for Minnesota Public Radio and wanted it only from behind. Then another from the Upper Peninsula who rode a bike and ate food out of a dumpster and shaved her hair on one side of her head but everything else she left natural. Then a petite comedienne who told me I had the best pictures and rode her bicycle to me in the suburbs. She brought cookies and gave me a long hug after we finished and said, "I needed that," before she left the house. Then another who had just returned from France. She lived in Eden Prairie with her parents and she said her dad was a police officer as she rested on my chest.

Then another who owned a flower shop and was once married to a genius but said the sex was "fucking horrible." She ate things I didn't know how to pronounce and did yoga and smelled of the spices grown on her rooftop garden. Then someone who came from a farming community in rural Minnesota and had pictures from her past year in Thailand. The word "Believe" was tattooed on her wrist and she kissed like an eel moves. Then another who hula-hooped and worked as a flight attendant and wore clothes they wore in the 50s. Her thighs were tan and meaty.

Then at last I met the one with the mad wild heart. In her profile picture her hair was like a pompom, and in another she gazed at an ocean from atop a ledge near mountains. In another she stood by her bike in a garden with frost on the ground. She had dark eyebrows. After a month, she replied.

"What I lacked in response time I'll more than make up for in smiles!" There was a joyful and genuine spirit in her, even online. It would only be better in person.

We met on a Friday night and came bounding up in her jalopy over the hump of the sidewalk. She was right, soon as she got out, she started to smile. She looked like a pale stick with a mop of black coils on her head, in a white dress with flower patterns, cut out on the sides. She moved with a bounce in her step that summer evening. We hugged hello. It was like she glowed as she told me her life story over pho.

MadWildHearts was born Madelyn and her grandparents founded a car wash in St. Paul and later divorced. Her grandfather remarried and now lives with the teller at that car wash who was 16 when they met. Madelyn's father, who for a long time installed cruise control systems in semi-trucks, now lives with her mom and her mom's boyfriend in their basement in Wisconsin. Madelyn worked at that car wash until she went to a private college in Ohio, one established a hundred years before but shut down her second semester.

"I took that as a sign I should travel." So Madelyn did, first with her boyfriend as they hitchhiked to Mexico, then back to Minnesota to work again at the car wash while she made "Minnesota Nice" t-shirts. She used that money to travel, moving down the east coast after putting an ad on the internet looking for anyone who needed an extra worker on their boat. She and her boyfriend ended up in Guatemala. There, Madelyn fell in love with another.

"I can stop talking," Madelyn told me in the restaurant.

"No," I said. "This is interesting, just don't tell me about which positions you were in."

"Oh yeah, so I was upside down…no, no just kidding." Madelyn laughed and told me how she came back to Minnesota after Guatemala and made more money at the car wash, then to China, then Cambodia, then other places in Southeast Asia, then back to the car wash, then to New Orleans where she lived with her sister and sold pot brownies on the street wearing a tutu while calling herself The Cookie Lady.

"Man," I said. "I never knew I was so boring."

"Oh no no," Madelyn said, "I think you're great." And I believed that.

After I paid, in my car, windows rolled down, Madelyn noticed my automatic drive, of all things.

"Can you drive stick?" she asked, and I told her about my days in high school when I worked as a janitor in the summer. I drove a van with a stick shift connected to the steering column.

"Three on the tree, " I said, which made her curious. Madelyn looked it up on her phone, showing me different pictures, asking if it was like this or that.

Then she asked, phone in hand, "So my friend has this comedy show at the Corner Bar, you wanna go?"

Yes I did, and we held hands over the center console as I drove us there. Madelyn was my champion as she helped me find a parking spot so close. I parallel-parked like I had never parallel-parked before. We embraced and made out in the car. Inside, with beers, we sat in front as Madelyn apologized for watching the screen— showing experimental comedy film clips on a loop— instead of talking with me. Why would she worry? We would talk for the rest of our lives.

After the show, Madelyn waited as I went to the bathroom. When I got out, I saw her near a tall man in a suit. They had just been laughing, but I didn't ask. It didn't matter. Nothing mattered, not anymore. Back in the car, I played her songs by a Parisian female singer.

"This is nice," Madelyn said, engulfed in the passenger seat. She was small and beginning to yawn. "Sorry, I get quiet when I get tired."

"That's okay," I said, because how many nights would I take her home after a long evening of laughs and new friends? I thought of that, scolded myself for thinking it, but thought it again, because I couldn't stop. We had parked back at the pho place. It was time for her to go.

"You're a good storyteller," I was saying. "Let's see each other whenever we can." I never said it that way before. A change of pace. A change of life.

"Mmhmm," she said, and I dove across the expanse, kissing her.

When we finished, Madelyn hopped out my car and got into hers. Ahead in her driver's seat, my headlights made a shadow of her mop-top. Diesel fumes coughed out the exhaust as she left, oblivious to the mess trailing behind her. We talked on the phone that night, and how good that was. The next afternoon I asked her out, and by midnight Madelyn had responded. Her apology for any misunderstanding took up five screens.

CHAPTER TWENTY-EIGHT

I need to be honest. I am not a delicate and bruised fruit. Hannah met my parents not long after I thought I had cancer. I told her they were coming to visit, and I said she should meet them. I didn't cloak that fact to make myself look better. I do this all the time, say things to make myself look better. But, in fact, no girl had ever met my parents before.

By the time Hannah met them, I had just begun to understand how a significant other can alleviate pressure from a family. Fewer questions and silent wonderings, no longer does one need to be evasive when their parents visit. With Hannah, I saw what it could be like to be normal. Having her, interactions would be effortless. It was like a destitute person having a long-wanted luxury they finally could afford.

On the day of their arrival, Hannah and I waited in the lobby of a Holiday Inn, a little farther out from where I lived in the suburbs. Hannah wore a blue dress, and her hair was dark as coal. She gave me her smile as she squeezed my hand. My parents came down from their room, and my dad soon inundated Hannah with jokes. My mom slapped his shoulder at the end of each one. Hannah liked all the attention, I could tell by her eyes, ever so often glancing at mine. I stood there thinking, how many years had I missed something as great and simple as this?

After the introductions, we went for a tour of the city. Hannah sat in the front seat while my parents sat in the back. Hannah gave the directions with her caring, soft voice. And though I haven't asked my mother or father since, nor would I ever, I believe they were content that day. They did not want a single thing more for me. Hannah pointed out the landmarks around downtown, and after that we went by the lakes in the residential areas. On the way to the suburbs we drove through Uptown, the youth neighborhood, where Hannah spotted a man and a woman, both of them wearing jeans rolled up to their ankles pushing single geared monochrome bikes. Though even after she explained to my parents what a hipster was, I don't think they understood.

"Weird," is all my father said, which made Hannah and I laugh and my mom slapped my dad's thigh. But

I don't think any of us argued. Weird was the most apt description.

Back at the hotel, Hannah and I swam in the pool. She wore her suit, a red two-piece with white polka dots where the bottom went almost up to her bellybutton. A tan woman with a large sexual nose and soft dark hair, I knew if anyone else walked by the pool, they would notice her. I was beyond proud.

After swimming, we showered and dressed and went to the hotel restaurant for supper. I don't think my parents asked me one question for the entire meal. It was the best dinner I had with them in years. They asked about Hannah, her art, what she planned to do for the upcoming semester, even the caricature work she did at fairs in the summer. Hannah told them about working part-time at the university, overseeing the CNC router, the fair jobs. My parents were not accustomed to knowing a working artist, and neither was I, but I think my mother, in particular, slowly relinquished doubt as Hannah spoke. Hannah was so professional about the way she explained everything.

In the lobby, after my dad paid, my parents hugged Hannah goodbye, and I cannot forget their embraces, no matter how much I try. It was the next weeks in my parents absence that demonstrated how little Hannah and I belonged together. Other couples must know this too, being happiest when not alone: when friends are around, or the offspring they have produced distracts them, or, like with me and Hannah, when parents are visiting. Because when we would go to the beach, all I could do was dream of other women, in other suits, wondering if they knew me the way I thought I was supposed to be known.

So I reactivated my profile, and I didn't hide it, and on break from the drug assembly line job one night, I got the text. "Do we need to talk?"

At home, I wrote Hannah an email. We had been together for nearly a year, and that's all I did. It washed away every portion of goodness Hannah Cohen once saw in me. Whatever she detected, the thing I believed was there and had always been disappointed when others didn't notice, was gone.

I fear I blinded her, the one person who ever saw me.

CHAPTER TWENTY-NINE

Much later, I quit the bookstore. I stopped writing poetry as well. I eventually understood that only a thin strand of people are interested in my kind of writing. And it seems, though I am mush in the presence of those types, I have never been long-haired enough, bearded enough, or smoked enough cigarettes to inspire their love. I've become older as well. I am too square for one of those. It no longer makes any sense. My writing never saved a life. It never fed the hungry.

Besides, for a good while, I didn't need it. Megan, the one who walked around the lake with me, she was my first online date in quite some time. In the interim, I improved as a man. I lost weight. I stopped drinking as much. I moved out of the suburbs and found a place in the city, even if it was a bit above my price range. Though I did something to combat that. I got my job back at the factory. I had to work my way back to the middle, but I took it, along with the overtime. Maybe my life only consisted of working—sometimes until three or four in the morning—but I didn't mind. The lack of having heartbreak outweighed the lack of having anyone.

It must have been my solo trip to Spain that doomed me. I had wanted to go ever since the Barcelona Olympics, and it was more or less what I thought it would be, or even more. I couldn't keep count of how many times I fell in love. So when I got back, I re-upped my profile, this time with stories of adventure. I described my new place in the artier section of Minneapolis, alongside new pictures, beside a newly purchased car. No more talk of quixotic aspirations. I was in my thirties. Time to act like it.

Then came Megan, the cyclist, the one whose back I massaged on the beach, with the athletic body and Wisconsin accent. She was the first I met in the new world. And with how it went, like it always had gone, others now might understand why someone like her — who I did not know—could break me so easily. It's also possible they might not. Every heart is a mystery.

CHAPTER THIRTY

Later still, in the summer, the evening of an arts festival in Minneapolis. Hannah, I have read, will be featured. Her words will span a bridge. And though I am glad to have a reason to get off the couch, I am nervous. This is going to be the first time seeing her in a long time. But I go, and I think the best thing will be for us not to see each other. I will admire her work. I will see the big letters on the bridge lighting up the dark—BELIEVE AND HOPE AND HOPE AND BELIEVE—then I'll go home.

Downtown now, and I start to notice small packs of artists. These young people push bikes and laugh. Their world is carefree. Through the steel and glass of the tall buildings, I get closer still. I don't know what it is, but something good will happen. I can sense that. I know Hannah has a boyfriend. Almost 40, a deejay, he has a beard and wears suit jackets and different colored jeans. My old landlord said, after I showed a picture of the man, "He's an older version of you, doesn't that make you feel good?"

If it did or did not, I could not say, but as I arrive at the stone bridge, I see there is no way we will meet. There are so many people, more than I anticipated by a long shot, all of them mixing around, buzzing with a night of art and community. Many stand on the bridge as I walk down the graded sidewalk, condos on either side of me. I see a sliver of one of Hannah's letters now, and a swell of pride comes over me. I survey the best way to get a full view. I take another step. Then I take another. A few more and I nearly walk into her.

Hannah turns, and I notice her makeup first—I don't think I ever saw her wear that much. She wears a pale blue dress, more subdued than anything she wore when we were together, and her boyfriend is here, so is her sister, who I also recognize. The boyfriend checks his phone, looking up for a second to glare at me. Her sister might strike me. Hannah seems confused. I can't blame her.

"Hannah," I say, my voice wavering. "How's it going?"

"Fine," she says.

"Boy," I say, pretending to look around. "Lotta people here. Didn't think I'd see you here with so many people." I regroup and do my best to squirm my way out of his. "So is there a better place to see everything?"

"Over there." Hannah points far away, to the east.

"Cool. I'll probably just go check it out then."

Hannah smiles, one not so different from when I first saw her when we ate pancakes. Her boyfriend and sister do not say a word, and I walk away like I have been spun on a top. Let loose, I stagger to where Hannah pointed, not thinking anything and everything at once.

Sitting down, I find myself on a patch of grass along the Mississippi River. Hannah is right, from here I see the letters well, flickering on as the sun goes down. The water becomes blacker. On the stone bridge a marching band plays and I stare at the glowing words, believe and hope. I should be extracting meaning from them. I should frame them in some way.

But I do not want to learn anything. I am looking at those words as a person separated from every person I have ever tried to love. That is such a failure; I don't know how to make sense of it.

ACKNOWLEDGMENTS

Thank you Raulie Ruiz, Matt Hardy, and Mary Juhl for your generous patience and guidance. This book was also made possible by kind folks with willing ears like Dan Flies, Kyle VanMiddlesworth, Erik Hadland, and Jenny Aron. The cover of this book was created by Elizabeth Anderson, a talented artist who deserves more credit than I give in such a small space. And to Joanne, my love, who is everything.

www.ingramcontent.com/pod-product-compliance
Lightning Source LLC
Chambersburg PA
CBHW021233130626
46554CB00004B/1477

* 9 780692 481226 *